THE KING'S SEER

BLESSED MOON

BOOK 2

D1525581

L.S. BETHEL

CHAPTER ONE

Serenity was bored. Her bottom was getting sore from sitting on her throne so long. It wasn't like she was purposely tuning out. Everyone was speaking in a language she had yet to master, so following the conversation was incredibly difficult. She'd given up twenty minutes in. She really wanted to skip the meeting and defer it all to her husband, but ever since her injury on the battlefield, he refused to let her out of his sight. It was endearing but also incredibly annoying. She'd much rather be helping her mother-in-law and making herself useful than be trapped in a room unable to listen to or give input on anything that was said. Interestingly, that was probably one of the few negatives involving her injury. There were several positive aspects of it as well.

One was that the eyes of the palace that once observed her with skepticism, now gaze at her welcomingly. Disdain gave way begrudgingly to respect, and genuine hatred turned to ignoring her; which she took as a win. Apparently, all she needed to do to earn the respect of the people was be willing to risk her life for the King.

Serenity felt her head start to droop for the fourth time before she jerked herself up, causing her to irritate her injury. She let out a small hiss, which drew Kang-Dae's attention.

"What's wrong? Are you in pain?" he asked completely derailing his briefing. Everyone's eyes were on her now. Feeling embarrassed at having the attention of the room, Serenity decided to take the opportunity to make an escape.

"I think I'm going to go back to the room," she said pushing herself off the throne. Kang-Dae jumped up.

"I will take you."

"You're in the middle of a meeting. Stay. Jung-Soo will walk me," she asserted.

"We will continue this discussion another time," he announced completely ignoring her.

She pulled on his arm and, in a hushed tone, spoke in his ear, "You wanted to be king so you could lead things like this. I'm just going back to the room. I'll be fine."

He was silent for a good two seconds before calling out, "Dismissed!" Serenity frowned and her irritation rose. This was both the negative and positive of what she had suffered. Positive because of Kang-Dae's special attention to her, which was nice- in most instances. It still gave her butterflies thinking of how he insisted on being the one to change the dressing on her injury and how gentle his touch was.

One week ago

Serenity winced again. Kang-Dae was applying medical apprentice Mehdi's salve to her still healing wound. Amoli usually helped her with this, but for some reason he insisted on doing it this morning. "Sorry," he said with sympathetic eyes. Serenity shook her head to signify she was alright. "Perhaps this pain will deter you from being so reckless," he said. Serenity's mouth dropped open in disbelief.

"Excuse me, I believe my recklessness saved you," she reminded him.

"There is no way to know that for sure. It's entirely possible the arrow would have just wounded me," he said in an annoyingly condescending tone. He seemed to enjoy the shocked look on her face.

"I-, You-," she stammered as Kang-Dae grinned. Realizing he was joking Serenity pushed at his shoulder, but the movement made her hiss. "Ow!"

"Do you enjoy causing yourself pain?" He admonished before gently blowing on her stinging wound. Him being so close to her exposed shoulder made her heart jump. His warm breath on her chest filled her with butterflies.

"No," she answered having a hard time forming the word. He helped redress the bandages. Every swipe of his fingers on her bare skin causing her to shiver. She hoped he didn't notice, mortified at her reaction to such a small thing.

"I will help you with this from now on. I do not want you to have to wait for Amoli to finish her morning duties."

"It's fine," she told him, but he shook his head. "I am here and am willing. I think helping his wife after she injures herself saving his life is the least a husband can do for such a woman." Serenity was so glad for her darker *skin, knowing if it wasn't, her face would be beet red. Once the bandage was secured, he pulled her dress back into place.*

"Thank you," she said, barely able to look him in the eyes. He smiled before placing a kiss on her forehead. "You are welcome Neeco."

Serenity felt heat rise to her cheeks at the memory. Kang-Dae's gentleness with her was a definite positive. The negative repercussions were that he was treating her like she was incapable of being without him. Today was not the first time he'd put her ahead of his duties, even when she'd insisted, she was fine. Just the other day Advisor Min had come into his study where she'd been, sitting in his chair at his insistence. Min had wanted Kang-Dae to meet with a possible new council member, to replace the late Amin. Kang-Dae was okay with it until Min mentioned the man had invited him to his home outside the city. Kang-Dae had quickly declined. He didn't vocalize it, but it was obvious to both Min and her he did not want to leave her on her own.

'Okay, I am officially tired of this.' Serenity thought as the men filed out. She noticed Jung-Soo lingering.

"You can leave as well," Kang-Dae said coldly. Jung-Soo lowered his head and obliged. That was one of the other major drawbacks of her injury. Kang-Dae still held some resentment for his friend for that day. He would barely speak to him and when he did, it was with an impersonal and sometimes angry tone. Not only that, Kang-Dae no longer felt safe leaving her in Jung-Soo's care. With Kang-Dae always dragging her off with him she hadn't been able to spend any time with Jung-Soo. She missed her friend. She hated to see the two at odds. She couldn't help feeling guilty knowing she was the cause.

Serenity stomped into the room with Kang-Dae hot on her trail. She'd sped walked the entire way refusing to acknowledge him. She angrily ripped off her gold headdress and practically slammed it on the vanity. She fumbled with the chain on her pink outer dress and a pair of strong hands moved to help unlock it, only for her to smack them away. She shrugged off the clothing ignoring her pain and faced Kang-Dae with a glare.

"This is going to stop." Serenity watched him with his faux innocent face and soft eyes trying to appear as if he had no idea where her anger came from. She was not going to fall for it. There was a cunning manipulator beneath those eyes. "I am not a child that you need to watch all the time."

"I only mean to make sure you are safe and well taken care of."

"I'm in the palace, not a battlefield. I don't think I have to worry about arrows here," she argued with a huff.

"Have you forgotten you were poisoned right on these grounds?" Serenity's jaw slackened. "Two times now your life has been at risk. You expect me to just do nothing? Feel nothing?" Serenity felt her irritation die down at the sincerity in his tone. She walked over to him.

"The whole point of marrying me was so that something like that wouldn't happen again," she reminded him softly.

"Even still, you think I can just sit by and not do anything to keep you from suffering those things? Neither can I leave you alone without you putting yourself in a dire situation." He let out a listless laugh. "Even Jung-Soo cannot be trusted to do what is necessary."

"Kang-Dae! I told you it wasn't his fault. You're his king, but I'm also his queen. I gave him an order and he followed it. Besides, you should be thankful."

"Thankful?" he scoffed brow raised, his skepticism obvious.

"Yes, thankful! You think I would've stayed put just because he refused to let me go with him? Like I was just gonna sit by and-," she paused as she realized she was repeating his own words back to him. The room was uncomfortably quiet. Serenity suddenly found something interesting to look at on the floor. Kang-Dae was attempting not to let his happiness at her slip-up show.

Serenity shook her head and sighed out in defeat. "I'm sorry that I scared you and I promise from now on to be more careful, so you don't have to worry as much." He looked to be about to interrupt so she quickly continued.

"In keeping with that, I will allow you one stipulation for me that will make you feel comfortable."

"Stipulation?" he asked unfamiliar with the word.

"You get one request that I will follow," she clarified.

Kang-Dae thought for a moment. "A personal guard. I should have appointed you one long ago. If you accept a personal guard to be with you at all times when I am not around, I will *attempt* to give you more freedom."

"How about just when I leave the palace?" Serenity offered.

"All times."

"Whenever I go outside?"

"All times."

"They go where I go but they stay outside the room," she settled on, not prepared to bend anymore.

Sensing her resolve Kang-Dae finally agreed, "fine."

"Fine."

Serenity pressed her lips together to keep from smiling. "Do I get to pick them out myself?"

"I'll ask Jung-Soo who he feels will be capable," Kang-Dae answered. Serenity was pleased to hear him speaking of Jung-Soo without his usual annoyance.

"Glad that's settled," she quipped before attempting to walk off.

"Where are you going?"

"To thank God. He just granted me a miracle," she joked as she headed toward the balcony.

CHAPTER TWO

"In waiting to act, that witch has been gaining the approval of the people and the nobles," the man spat. It made him sick to hear the murmurs in the palace about how brave and loyal the new Queen was. How could they not see her for the infiltrator she was?

"Calm yourself," his partner spoke.

"He's right. Every moment we wait it will be even harder to remove her," the female spoke up.

"Did you forget what happened to Amin when he tried, and that was before there was a crown on her head? No, we have to be smart. Our hands must not be a part of it. The best way is to use hands not our own."

"Is that not what Amin did?"

"Amin used the wrong hands."

****

"One at a time!" Serenity scolded in Xianian. Posted at the edge of the marketplace, soldiers formed a protective barrier as they stood by the packed carts. The gaggle of children calmed for just a moment before continuing to push each other out of the way. "Hey!" she shouted. They all quieted. "Everyone will get some. But if you fight, I will send you back with nothing," she warned. Like magic, the kids formed an orderly line as they waited patiently for their provisions. Amoli smiled at the sight. Serenity, in an effort to help those in need, had decided to hand out supplies to the impoverished children in the city. With the food shortage, she knew they would be suffering the most as they had no means to pay for regular priced food- let alone the now much more expensive kind.

Serenity had gone to the Queen Dowager with the idea, at which she had eagerly approved, stating the people would greatly appreciate it. Serenity, Amoli, and a few ladies oversaw the giving while the palace workers gave out sacks with vegetables, fruit, and bread.

"Do not eat it all too fast. We'll be back again soon with more." She told them. The kids cheered and rushed up to hug her. Arezoo- the head of her new guard- stepped up to force them back, but Serenity stopped her, insisting it was fine. When Jung-Soo first introduced her, she had been pleased to see a familiar face. Like Amoli, Arezoo hailed from a region where English was spoken regularly, which was one of the reasons Jung-Soo had chosen her. The other two, Nasreen and Gyuri, she'd never seen. Nasreen was the younger sister to Arezoo. Though they shared the same eyes, the resemblance stopped there. Whereas Arezoo kept her hair shorter, Nasreen's long brown hair was in a braid tossed over her right shoulder. Her big round eyes were contrary to Arezoo's smaller ones. Where Arezoo was hard and gave off a tough persona, Nasreen looked soft and sweet. However, Jung-Soo assured her she was incredibly deadly. Gyuri was actually from a noble family. With hair always pinned to the top of her head, strong facial features, robust build, and dark brows, no one would have ever guessed she was once a noble lady. However, she had wanted to be a soldier so badly she renounced her title and enlisted. Gyuri had requested to be a part of her guard. Apparently, she was very eager to serve a Queen who would brave a battlefield. Serenity didn't have the heart to tell her she'd been terrified the whole time.

Serenity gave as many of the kids she could reach a hug feeling a great amount of joy to have made them so happy. She was reminded of the children she once taught and the fulfillment she got from working with them. One by one the kids ran off. Serenity and the others began to pack up, but a loud crash startled them all; except for her guard who already had their weapons out. Loud arguing could be heard from around the corner within the marketplace. Serenity started to walk over only for Arezoo to block her path. "It's not safe," she warned.

"That's why I have you," she said smartly before walking around her. Her guard quickly surrounded her as she walked towards the rising voices. A small group of people was yelling at a man standing in front of his broken cart. Scattered pieces of vegetables littered the ground. The man was screaming at the crowd brandishing a large potato at them as if it were a weapon.

Using her best "teacher" voice Serenity called out in Xianian, "What is going on here?" The crowd and the man stopped their fighting and dropped to their knees to bow. "You can stand," she told them. They all got back to their feet and Serenity repeated her question, starting another bout of screaming. Serenity did her best to listen, but they were talking way too fast and over each other. She wasn't able to pick out anything useful.

"Amoli?" she asked looking to her friend for help.

"I believe these people are upset at this man because he has been purposely increasing his prices so high no one can afford them. He's the only merchant in the market who sells produce of good quality," Amoli told her.

The man spoke out angrily and Amoli relayed, "he says he must put himself through dangerous situations to get the food here as he is the only one capable of sneaking through the blockade. He feels the prices are more than fair due to his sacrifice."

Serenity held up her hand quieting the merchant and the crowd. She waved the merchant over. He shuffled toward her hesitantly. "You can get through the blockade?" she asked. He nodded. Asking Amoli to translate she continued, "Would you like me to assign you a personal escort to protect you and help you bring in more food?

More food means more profit." The man nodded eagerly, saying thank you.

"But you need to make sure the prices stay reasonable," she added. The merchant looked offended at the idea. "The blockade will end one day. When it does, there will be more merchants with produce just as good as yours. Do you want people to remember you as the one who took advantage of the Kingdom's misfortune, or the one who helped the people through it?" The implication of her words must have hit him because he went to his knees asking for forgiveness. Serenity removed one of her rings and placed it on the ground before him.

"I will pay for these people's things today," she said. Amoli looked surprisingly at her even as she translated, and the crowd gasped. The merchant took the ring and started bowing profusely expressing his thanks and apologies. The crowd called out to her with words of thanks. Serenity accepted their gratitude with a smile. She had to admit, there was a great deal of satisfaction in ruling when things worked out. Going back to being a regular teacher might be boring after this. Serenity was eager to return to the palace and tell Kang-Dae about what had happened.

On their way back, Amoli sat in the carriage with her. "May I speak candidly, my Queen?" she asked.

"You don't need to ask that Amoli. You're my friend. You're one of the only people I can talk to candidly." Amoli smiled at that.

"I just wanted to tell you I think you are doing well. You may not realize it yet, but being the Queen suits you," she told her. Serenity grinned.

"I still think there are way more qualified people than me, but thank you."

CHAPTER THREE

Serenity's good mood lasted all of twenty minutes

when she returned to the palace. Knowing Kang-Dae was

busy with his own affairs, she decided to get in some

studying. As she sat in her office practicing her phrases, a

knock sounded and Advisor Min entered. "May I have a

word, my Queen?" he asked. Serenity released a sigh and

put her book down. Advisor Min was one of those people

who offered her just enough respect to avoid appearing

defiant. Though his attitude improved slightly after the

arrow incident, he still stared at her suspiciously as if he

was waiting for her "true colors" to show any moment.

"What is it?" she asked.

"I heard you had some issues in the marketplace."

Serenity rolled her eyes. One of the women must've been

someone he put near her to keep an eye on her and reported back what had happened.

"If you're going to continue to assigning spies to my detail, I'd appreciate it if you would just tell me."

Ignoring her, he continued on. "It would be best to adhere to all market issues to me or the King."

"Any particular reason?" She asked looking back down at her book.

"The market is delicate, especially given the current state of trade. These things should be handled by those who have experience dealing with such situations."

"I think I handled it just fine," she said with a tight smile.

"Possibly, but you also could have cost the people a much-needed food source."

"But I didn't" she countered. "Or is that what's bothering you? Not that I'm doing the job, but that I'm doing it well. It puts a whole wrinkle in your "she's evil" theory, huh?"

Advisor Min didn't respond, not that she expected him to. Serenity turned her attention back to her book.

"As long as I'm here, and as long as I'm Queen, I'm going to do my best to make sure I'm taking care of this country. If I need your help or advice, I will be sure to ask for it."

"Did you consider the danger you put yourself in and how it would affect our King if you had been hurt?" Min countered. With a roll of her eyes and a loud sigh, she shut her book.

"I wasn't and he doesn't need to know about that part." Min just stared, his posture going tight. "You already told him, didn't you?" As if on cue, her door flew open.

Kang-Dae appeared dressed in a white shirt covered with a sleeveless blue robe and blue pants. Like the snitch he was, Min slinked out the room to avoid the storm he started.

"You promised," Kang-Dae started coming toward her. "You said you would be careful."

Serenity let out a groan. "I was. My guard was with me the whole time. I was never in danger."

"You could have been," he countered.

"I wasn't."

"You had no way of knowing that. There are more dangers beyond these walls than you can imagine," he told her.

"Are you sure about that? I'm pretty sure I've almost died more here than out there."

Her joke was not well received. Since humor was not working, she tried a different tactic.

"If I had sensed anything, I would never have done it. There were no visions; no bad feelings. The only thing I knew was that the people were unhappy, and I wanted to help. So, I did."

Kang-Dae didn't appear too accepting of this. She stood and walked over to him. "Your Queen managed to win the hearts of the kids and adults of the city in one day. And she took steps that should bring more food into the capital." She smiled brightly at him batting her eyes. "Aren't you a little proud?" He looked away from her trying not to let her influence his mood. But she could tell his anger was already dissipating. "My King." She added in her sweetest voice. She saw a hint of a smile on his face before he quickly hid it beneath a scowl.

"Be more cautious next time," he grumbled.

"I will, my King," she said with a dramatic bow. Kang-Dae rolled his eyes before letting the smile he'd been fighting come through.

"Have you eaten yet?" She shook her head. "Come. You're done for the day." She beamed as he grabbed her hand and the two walked out together, not noticing the disapproving eyes of Min watching them. He thought about what he'd learned and his trepidation at revealing it. Now, it didn't seem like such a bad thing. Perhaps it was time to share what he'd found with his King.

CHAPTER FOUR

Serenity was flying. She soared above in the night sky looking down at the lands below her. She wasn't in Xian. She didn't know how she knew that, but she did. The land was plush with green fields and thick trees. As she looked closer, she saw giant fruit hanging off every one. She wanted to go down and grab some, but wasn't able to descend. A glow from below her caught her attention. Something was coating the ground, slowly moving through the land. It took Serenity a second to realize it was lava. Lava was flowing between the trees covering the grounds. However, every tree the lava touched didn't burn or even get scorched. Instead, as lava made its way throughout the forest, all the fruit increased in size. There were people in boats just drifting on the lava, but they didn't appear to be in any kind of danger. Each boat was filled with heaps of fruit. The people smiled brightly at first until they reached a dark part of the land. Their smiles turned and became full

of fear. The people began throwing their harvest into the

river of lava letting it flow with the current. The ground

began to rumble. The people did their best to stay aboard

their boats. As the rumbling continued, sorrow filled each

of their faces. The people in the boats only had one thing

left. Each one carried a small box, all with different

designs. The way they held it so carefully, it was obvious it

was precious to them. Eyes full of tears they dropped the

boxes into the river. A flash of lightning crackled in the

distance, and a massive figure could be seen-

"Serenity." Serenity's eyes opened and the first thing she saw was the concerned face of her husband. "You were unsettled. Was it a nightmare?" She shook her head as she groggily sat up.

"A vision." Kang-Dae helped her as she rose, pausing only a second at the mention of a vision.

"Tell me." Serenity slowly recounted what she saw as best she could.

"You spoke the word 'echang' when you woke."

"I did?" Serenity asked, not remembering that at all. Kang-Dae nodded.

"It wasn't familiar to me." Serenity was surprised to hear that. She knew only just enough Xian to get by. What word could she have said that Kang-Dae didn't know? "What do you think the dream meant?" he asked.

Taking a deep breath and releasing it, she lightly shook her head. "I'm not sure. Normally I would think lava was a bad thing, but it didn't seem like it in the dream. It was like it was helping the land grow more food." From her limited first-grade teacher science knowledge, she knew lands with volcanoes tended to be very fertile.

"Could your vision be trying to give us a solution to the food shortage?"

"Maybe. Although, I have no idea where that place could be. All we know about it is that it might have volcanos."

"Volcanos?" repeated Kang-Dae. "Could this land be an island?"

Serenity tried to recall her overhead flight in the dream. There were moments when she saw glimpses of the sea. "Possibly," she answered.

"Kah Mah."

"What?"

"Kah Mah, the Misty Island. It's an island off the southwest coast. It used to be a part of Xian."

"What happened?"

"Their leaders disagreed with my great grandfather's actions. They refused to serve him any longer and declared themselves an independent nation. Luckily for them, he died before he could force their submission," Kang-Dae explained.

"I've never heard you talk about your great-grandfather before. I don't think I've heard anyone even mention him since I've been here."

"There is good reason for that. He was quite... I guess the word you can use is, deranged. He caused an unnecessary war with the land we now call our southern province."

"That's where Kyril is from, isn't it?" she asked. Kang-Dae nodded. "They were once their own nation until great-grandfather felt disrespected by their chieftain. The chieftain was celebrating his daughter's engagement. Hearing how beautiful she was, Great grandfather felt insulted he didn't offer her as a potential wife for my grandfather. The chief would not apologize, of course, and great grandfather became furious. He ordered their absolute allegiance and they refused. So, he sent his army to wipe them out. They fought for years until they could no longer sustain themselves through it all and had to surrender. People were very happy when grandfather had taken a wife and became King. He was a much simpler man, but a better ruler in every aspect. He immediately gave their lands back and tried to help them rebuild. But the country had been so destroyed by the war they were unable to support themselves. To give them a better chance he made them a part of Xian so they could benefit from our resources until they could fend for themselves once more."

"Wow." That was all Serenity could say.

"Xian's history is not all pleasant, but we do learn from it. And as awful as it was without all of that, I would not have Kyril."

"Thank God for Kyril," Serenity proclaimed, knowing how much Kang-Dae relied on him.

"Mmm, the land is doing much better now. With the way things are, no one has felt a need to change anything."

"Was that the reason Kah Mah separated?"

"Mostly, they had been very close allies with the southern province, as their island was not far from them. They wanted to help but knew it was a losing battle. It wasn't until the chieftain's death that they rebelled. Once my grandfather was crowned, he let them be."

"If you're right about my vision, they may be who we need to go to."

"Xian hasn't interacted with Kah Mah for years. I fear it won't be easy creating an alliance on either end. There are still those here who feel that their actions were unforgivable, no matter the reason."

"Do you?" she asked curiously.

"I believe vows should be upheld until they go against what you know to be right. I cannot fault them for doing what they believed they must."

"Can you convince the council of that?"

"Me? Neeco, that is what I have you for." Serenity narrowed her eyes as he just grinned.

***

The King and Queen sat on their thrones overlooking the people before them. Representatives from the western and southern regions had come to petition the crown. They claimed their people were on the brink of starvation and wanted to beg the capital for help. Though the eastern province had been retaken, there was still a blockade separating most of the country from the much-needed farmlands. It was not enough to feed everyone.

"Please my King, my Queen, we can't go on like this much longer. Riots are breaking out almost every week. Thieves are running rampant. Our cities are on the brink of collapse."

"Unfortunately, we do not have the resources to offer any more than we already have," Satori spoke. "Giving more to you would just be taking more from someone else."

Serenity looked to Kang-Dae who just stared back expectantly. She rolled her eyes before speaking.

"What about Misty Island?" Serenity asked suddenly. Everyone looked over to her.

"I had a vision about them last night. I believe they can help us," she informed them.

"We do not trade with Kah Mah," Satori responded. "They have long since abandoned us."

"My Queen, you may not understand, but I assure you there are reasons-," Yoon began to add.

"Everyone has reasons. But this isn't about the past-it's about Xian's future."

"And those reasons are insignificant at the moment." Kang-Dae continued for her.

"With respect, my King, I do not believe turning against your king is an insignificant act," stated Satori.

"No, it isn't. But neither is inciting a war for personal reasons," Serenity pointed out.

"How da-," one look from Kang-Dae shut Yoon up quickly.

"You were saying?" Kang-Dae asked slowly, the threatening edge of his tone not going unnoticed.

"Nothing, my King." After a short tense silence, the conversation continued.

"Regardless of their reason, we cannot look to those who so easily break their vows for help. How can we trust them to uphold their end?" Satori asked.

Serenity thought that was a fair point. She didn't know much or anything about these people. But clearly, her dream knew something she didn't. So, she chose to trust it.

"Trust takes time to rebuild. This can be an opportunity to do just that."

"My Queen," Satori bit out. He always said it like it pained him to even utter the words. "This should not be taken lightly."

"Our people suffer," stated Kang-Dae. "If we are unwilling to do everything in our power to stop it, how can we claim to be working in their best interest?" Kang-Dae questioned. No one said a word. Kang-Dae looked at Advisor Min. "Have an envoy sent there as soon as possible, so we can open negotiations." Min bowed and left the room. "As soon as we have made a deal, we will get the food out to both your provinces," Kang-Dae assured the representatives. They bowed in gratitude.

CHAPTER FIVE

After the day was done, Kang-Dae lay upright in bed reading while sneaking glances at Serenity, who was doing her strange ritual of wrapping her hair up in silk. She had told him once it was something she did to keep her hair from getting too dry. He didn't understand it, but he took her word for it.

"How exactly can you read without looking at the book?" Serenity teased, repeating the same words he'd said to her once before. Kang-Dae chuckled before shutting the book.

"I guess I am just in awe of how amazing my Queen is," he answered honestly. She smiled bashfully.

"You know, back home women call themselves queens for doing the smallest things. Here I am a real queen, and I can truly say I slay." He laughed at her confusing jargon. "Rielle was always-," she stopped short.

Kang-Dae could see the joy turn to sadness right before his eyes.

"What is it?" he asked concerned. She blew out the lantern by her mirror and stood.

"Nothing," she said, getting on her side of the bed presenting her back to him. Completely unsatisfied with the answer and her change in demeanor, he reached over and turned her so she was facing him.

"You told me you would no longer keep things from me." A guilty looked passed through her. "Talk to me."

"I just… I realized I hadn't thought about them today, or yesterday."

Kang-Dae didn't need to ask who they were, knowing she was referring to those she left behind. Serenity played with her necklace. He noticed she did that whenever she thought of her family. He imagined it was because it was her only connection to her home. "I feel guilty because I know they must be worried. My mom cried for a day when I got lost once. I was missing for an hour. I can't even imagine what she's feeling now. My dad," her voice cracked. "He used to drink. He stopped when he realized it was getting bad. I worry he might start up again all because of me. Rielle, my best friend, her life is constantly messy. I was worried about her even when I saw her all the time, but I always knew she'd come to me whenever she needed me. But now I'm not there. I have all these people probably thinking I'm dead and I'm just over here, absolutely fine. When I start to feel happy, I remember what they might be going through, and I feel guilty." A tear rolled down the bridge of her nose.

Kang-Dae moved so that they were face to face. "When you get back, all those fears and worries will be forgotten," he assured her. "I will go see Min tomorrow to check on his progress. If he still hasn't found anything, I will go to that village myself." He promised. He took her hand in his. "I will get you back, I swear." She nodded through her tears.

"Thank you."

"Sleep." He ordered softly. She nodded and lay down facing him, and he did the same. Her eyes slowly began to droop before they finally fluttered shut.

He stayed awake watching her, even after she fell asleep. He found himself doing that a lot lately. He'd grown used to her presence in his life. When he'd taken her as his wife for her safety, he didn't know how their relationship would grow. Before he realized she wasn't completely mad and revealed herself to be a seer, he figured they could develop a fondness for one another with time. When it became obvious that time would not be necessary to build his feelings for her, he hoped she would feel the same. The moment he found out she truly was from another world, those hopes had been dashed for he knew he would have to keep his promise to help her return. However, since the day she had willingly taken an arrow for him, things between them felt as though they were flourishing, but tonight was his reminder that things were not that simple. He'd gotten too comfortable, refusing to think about what was to come. It was strange to think that he could become so attached to someone who only entered his life a few months ago. He'd never admit it aloud to her, but if it turned out he could not help her return, he knew a part of him would not be disappointed.

***

"You came alone? Is your daughter having second thoughts?" The conspirator asked. Since he had approached the man with his intentions, he'd immediately involved his daughter claiming she would be eager to help. He'd yet to meet with him without her.

Yoon shook his head. "I had to. It's best if she were not a part of this portion of the plan. She would not agree to this. She still cares for him. It's better if she doesn't know. She doesn't need to know the details to play her part. Did you get it?"

"Yes. It's already been made. We just need the right opportunity to plant it."

"How long will it take to take effect?" Yoon asked.

"There's no way of knowing, it depends on the person. But it will do its job. That is certain." The conspirator answered.

"We can't be sure that witch won't see this coming," Yoon said.

"From what we've heard, her visions are sporadic and vague. She never sees faces or even direct actions. Even if she does catch a glimpse of something, she wouldn't understand it. Her ignorance will be our advantage. By the time she figures it out, all of Xian will be against her."

***

Kang-Dae awoke to a warm hand in his. He smiled to see Serenity so close. Despite last night's woes, her face showed nothing but tranquility. He resisted the urge to run his thumb across her cheek, not wanting to wake her. He wanted to lay there and watch her as long as he was able, but he had a promise to keep. Kang-Dae meant it when he swore to Serenity to get her home despite the growing desire building in him for her to stay. He understood that this was not home to her. Not eager to do what he knew he should, he reluctantly got up. Carefully slipping from the bed, he quietly dressed himself before heading out. He went straight to his study right after sending word to have Min meet him there as soon as possible. He didn't come as quickly as he'd expected. In fact, Kang-Dae couldn't remember a time when Min didn't come as soon as he was called. It put him on edge. Was Min trying to avoid him? Now that he thought about it, it had been days since his advisor came to speak to him. After every council meeting, he was the first out of the doors. His head began to fill with all sorts of possibilities. Had he found nothing and was afraid of being reprimanded, or was it the opposite?

Min finally arrived in his usual simple attire. "My King," he greeted as he stood before him.

"Has there been any news from the village?" Judging from the way Min's body tensed, and his eyes shifted Kang-Dae could tell Min knew something. Kang-Dae became angry at the fact that he was keeping valuable information to himself. "Tell me," he demanded.

"I do not know the validity of this information," Min started. Kang-Dae was growing impatient and he silently urged Min to continue. "It seems the occurrence of those who appear on the lake's edge only happens on a certain day."

Kang-Dae's brow quipped up. "What day?"

"The night of the blessed moon. The villagers believe the night of the blessed moon can be used to channel great power. It's why all those who appear on that night are thought to be sorcerers or witches."

Kang-Dae thought carefully. If the moon was indeed the key, he may have just found Serenity her way home. He ignored the uncomfortable feeling that grew in his gut at the thought of her returning. His feelings were inconsequential. "We need to find out when the next blessed moon is." Min nodded quietly. "Have our scholars chart the skies."

"I will, my King," Min said not moving.

"Is there something else?" Kang-Dae asked. Min was silent.

"Min," Kang-Dae called out.

"No, no my King, there's nothing else." He bowed and quickly exited.

CHAPTER SIX

Serenity was knocked to the ground for the fifth

time. Her body was in pain and all she wanted was to give

in. "Arezoo, you're being too rough. She's our Queen."

Nasreen admonished her older sister.

"And she should know how to protect herself if the

time comes. Her opponents won't be as nice as me."

'Nice', Serenity thought bitterly. When she'd asked

Arezoo to teach her how to defend herself, she hadn't

expected the woman to be so…professional.

"It's okay," she groaned as she forced herself to

stand once more. Trying not to glare at her captain, she

brushed off her pants, which she was so grateful to be

wearing. Her workout clothes were so comfortable, it was

almost worth the beatings to have the chance to wear them.

Being Queen, she wasn't allowed to wear them outside the

practice room- them not being acceptable attire for royal women, apparently. The sleeveless white top she was wearing was as close to a tank top as she could get in this world.

"Clearly Arezoo has some personal issues with me and she's using this as an opportunity to share them," Serenity said dryly.

The corner of Arezoo's mouth curled up ever so slightly. "Of course not, my Queen. I merely want you to be prepared. If there is ever a moment we are not at your side, it would grant me peace to know you would not be helpless in the face of such danger." Despite her sore body Serenity was moved by her concern.

Just as Arezoo had shown her, she took a protective stance, keeping her arms up to block any upper attacks. Arezoo jerked forward and Serenity shuffled back two steps to avoid her. Arezoo nodded. "Good."

Serenity did not relax, as she had been fooled before. The pain in her left shoulder was a reminder to not let her guard down around this woman. "Hit me," Arezoo ordered.

"No, thank you," Serenity declined immediately, shaking her head.

"We have to work on more than just defensive techniques. You need to learn at least enough to stun your opponent so you can get away," Arezoo explained.

Uncertainty plastered all over her face, Serenity gave a reluctant nod before giving her best attempt at a right hook. Arezoo caught her fist easily. Moving freakishly fast, in Serenity's opinion, Arezoo spun behind her pinning Serenity's arm behind her back in a painful grip.

"Ow! Ow! Ow!" Serenity cried out.

"Don't go for the obvious target."

"Okay, okay, I got it!" Serenity conceded. Arezoo relinquished her hold. Cradling her now aching arm, Serenity pouted.

"A real opponent will not show mercy, so neither should you."

"I think she's doing very well," Kang-Dae's voice called out, startling only Serenity. The other two women jumped up to bow, but Kang-Dae held his hand up to stop them as he entered.

"You can leave us," he told them all, keeping his eyes fixed on Serenity. The women didn't hesitate to make themselves scarce and shut the door behind them.

"What's wrong?" Serenity asked once they were alone. She could tell something had happened. His eyes lacked their usual brightness when he was around her and his face carried a somber expression. Instead of answering, he reached for her hand and gently pulled her into his arms.

Serenity could barely breathe as he held her tightly around the waist, while his other hand cradled her head ever so gently to his chest. The way he was holding her made her stomach do somersaults. She felt safe, even precious in his arms, but the thought that something was probably wrong suddenly entered her mind. "You're scaring me a little bit," she admitted with a nervous laugh. Kang-Dae only tightened his hold. Serenity was officially worried. Whatever was causing him to act this way, she wasn't sure she wanted to know. After what seemed like forever, he finally allowed himself to release her.

He closed his eyes for a second and reopened them. "I spoke to Min," he said. Serenity felt her heart drop. Was this it? Was she about to hear that there was no way home for her? She swallowed past the painful lump in her throat. "And?" she asked, her voice quivering.

"The villagers believe that you and the others appeared on a very specific night. A night of a special moon." Serenity's brows drew together. "They believe whatever happened to you, could only happen on the night of that moon."

Serenity could feel her anxiety quickly decline. "So, theoretically, if I went to the lake on that night, I might be able to get back?" Kang-Dae looked down before nodding. Serenity released the breath she'd been holding. "Oh my God," she breathed. Suddenly overcome with happiness, she threw herself onto him wrapping her arms around his neck. In her head, she thanked God for answering her prayers. It was only when she noticed Kang-Dae wasn't hugging her back that she pulled away. Now, that somber look made sense to her. Guilt tore through her as she realized that in her happiness, he was hurting. Even in her joy, she recognized what he may be feeling because underneath her relief, she felt the same.

"Thank you," she said softly. "You don't know how much this means to me." Kang-Dae gave her a sad smile that didn't reach his eyes, which made her feel even worse.

"I do not have a date yet, but when I do I will let you know," he informed her before turning and rushing out of the room. Serenity wanted to call after him, but she stopped herself. She was essentially abandoning the poor man. If he needed space from her to deal with that, she should grant it. She figured it was probably for the best to distance herself. Maybe it would make their separation easier.

***

Min paced back and forth in his room. He wasn't sure what to do now. In his cowardice, he'd withheld vital information from his King. That alone was enough for him to lose his position and title. If he did not reveal what he knew, the consequences would be much graver for everyone. At the time he couldn't bring himself to say it. A part of him wondered whether it was for fear of his King's reaction or something else. Regardless, he knew he could not keep this to himself despite how he felt. He could only hope the King would be merciful.

CHAPTER SEVEN

Kyril circled a portion on the map as Kang-Dae watched. "This would be a good place to station men. The natural defenses of the land will give them an advantage if Katsuo's men come this route."

"Just stationing our men in places he may come isn't good enough. We would only overextend ourselves and give him the advantage. Our best defenses come with strategies that work best with greater numbers. We can't organize a good defense or offense when we decrease our men.

"Agreed, but if we can't hold them off, they will gain too much of our lands and we leave ourselves open to be surrounded."

Kyril was right as he usually was, but it didn't change the facts. They did not have enough men to defend every part of Xian. "Perhaps it's time we start going on the offensive."

"My King?"

"All our information comes once Katsuo has made a move in our lands. We need to get a step ahead of him," explained Kang-Dae.

"Like you said, we can't spare many. Sending in scouting teams to all the places Katsuo's men are said to be would be counterproductive," Kyril told him.

Kang-Dae smiled as he smoothed out a corner of the map. "We don't need to send out our men. We have millions of spies at our disposal."

Kyril tilted his head not understanding where Kang-Dae was going with this. "Katsuo is occupying our lands with our people. He's taking their food and terrorizing their towns. If we put out the word for them to send information about what they see and where, we can get a better idea of what Katsuo is up to."

Thoroughly impressed, Kyril nodded. "That could work. We'll let all the representatives know so they can spread the word in their lands." Kyril rolled up the map. "We can send out envoys this afternoon."

"Good. The sooner the better. He's been far too quiet lately, which means he's planning something. If we can strike first, we may be able to expel him from Xian once and for all."

A knock at the door had both men looking toward it. "Come," Kang-Dae called out.

Min entered slowly, eyes downcast. "What is it, Min?"

"I need a word with you my King," Min said softly. This was not like him at all. Even when Min was in disagreement with him, he usually offered his point of view

61

boldly without fear. Reading the room, Kyril decided to excuse himself.

At first, Kang-Dae was unsure as to what this could be about until he thought about his last order to Min. 'The blessed moon' he thought to himself.

"Do you have a date yet?"

"No, my King. But there's something else you need to know; something I didn't tell you." With narrowed eyes Kang-Dae awaited Min's confession, feeling no small amount of unease.

***

Kang-Dae didn't return to his shared room with Serenity until much later in the night. He closed the door quietly behind him. As expected, Serenity was fast asleep. Walking over to her side he looked down at her. He pulled the blanket up further on her, careful not to get any blood on her or it. Once he was satisfied she was comfortable, he went to the basin to wash his hands. When he was done, he made sure to pour out the used water now tinted pink. He placed a crude wrap around his hand to soothe the pain that he was barely feeling. After leaving a bleeding Min on his knees, Kang-Dae needed to clear his head. But the only thing occupying his mind was what had been revealed to him. Once he'd taken his anger out on Min for his omittance, he was left with a growing uncertainty. He sat in the chair across from the bed just thinking, never feeling more conflicted in his life than he did at that moment.

CHAPTER EIGHT

The King and Queen of Xian were acting strangely.

That's what those who watched them felt. It was obvious that something was different between them because they no longer acted as they once did. Where before they were constantly around one another- usually joking or conversing fondly; lately they were hardly seen together anymore. On those rare occasions, they would barely look at one another, let alone speak. People questioned what could have brought about such a drastic change. Whispers were beginning to spread around the palace. Rumors about nonexistent arguments, the King regretting his choice, and even possible infidelity were being discussed among the palace workers and nobility. The distance between them was off-putting to some, but others saw an opportunity.

"Do you think he has begun to see her for what she is?" Yoon asked feeling hopeful.

"Possibly," the conspirator answered. "We cannot know for sure."

"But this is the time, right? We should strike now before she can worm her way back into his graces," Jae-Hwa spoke. The man nodded.

"Yes, we must begin subtly. For now, we plant the seeds of doubt among them. We must keep them apart."

"I know what seeds to plant," the other man claimed, his face gleaming in the moonlight.

***

Kang-Dae left the room before Serenity woke up for the fourth time. He hadn't occupied the same space as her while she was conscious in days. He couldn't bring himself to look her in the eyes let alone speak to her, fearful of what would come out. Serenity was not much better. It appeared as though she was in on his plan to avoid her at all costs because she never questioned it. There were times when he'd miscalculated and almost ran into her, but it would be her who turned and went the other way.

Too distracted by the things going on in his mind, he found himself slacking when it came to his duties. He'd gone back to leaning on the council for such things. Satori had taken charge, delighted to once again have the power he had been denied for the past couple of months. His mother had not been happy to learn that, but even a scolding from her wasn't enough to break him out of the place he'd found himself in. He spent most of his days holed up in his study, with nothing but the burning lanterns to keep him company. Kang-Dae had mentally checked out and everyone saw it. There were very few who had the gall to do something about it.

Jung-Soo didn't knock or have himself announced as he entered into the King's study. Kang-Dae barely looked up from his desk, though there was nothing in front of him. Jung-Soo leaned up on the side, not having or caring to show even a modicum of propriety at the moment. "Fix it," was all he said.

"I can't."

"You're the King, and her husband. Fix it."

"I said I can't. There's nothing I can do that will make this better." Jung-Soo waited for him to continue, knowing he'd been keeping things in.

"She wants to go home." Jung-Soo only paused for a moment because he wasn't exactly surprised. Serenity had been very clear about her wants from the beginning. He knew there must have been more to it.

"Can she?"

"It's possible." Now things made more sense and Jung-Soo had to stamp down his own sadness so he could focus on his friend. If there was a chance for her to return, Kang-Dae would honor his vow to help her do so- no matter how he felt. Jung-Soo knew it must have been weighing heavily on him. Still, there was something in his eyes that made Jung-Soo think he was holding back. He wanted to prod, but he could feel that even releasing this much was hard for him. So, he let it go to focus on the more obvious.

"Have you considered asking her to stay?"

Kang-Dae slowly shook his head. "You know as well as do she won't. The most important thing to her is getting home to her family. She will do whatever it takes to get back to them," he spoke sadly.

"Seems to me things have a way of changing," Jung-Soo mused. "When she first arrived, her only thoughts were to get home. Now, she's putting herself in danger to keep you safe. She's running a kingdom. Maybe you can convince her that she could have a life here- a new home. Convince her to stay," Jung-Soo commanded, but was unsure how much of what he was saying was for Kang-Dae's benefit or his own.

Kang-Dae looked unsure. This was not an easy task. Serenity was excited to return to her family. It didn't appear she had any desire to make this place her home. The way she spoke about them, it was clear she loved them dearly. Kang-Dae doubted it had ever crossed her mind to stay, not when she had so much to return for.

"Are you unwilling to even try?" Jung-Soo challenged. His query seemed to spark something in him because Kang-Dae's expression slowly shifted from uncertainty to determination. 'Maybe there was hope after all,' Jung-Soo thought.

CHAPTER NINE

While Kang-Dae was busy putting off his

responsibilities, too distracted by their personal drama,

Serenity had done the opposite by throwing herself into

work. She oversaw the food distribution to the provinces,

which only annoyed Satori more. She had been prepared to

work with Min on it, but the man was nowhere to be found.

Amir had told her he was sick and would not be available

for a few days. It had been a bit odd to her as Min seemed

like the type to never take a break. She worked with the

temporary treasurer to figure out where they could afford to

cut spending to prepare for the coming season. She even

did some "public relations" by spending time with the

noblewomen of the court, getting them involved in the

kingdom's needs. That was the most uncomfortable

considering how nasty several of those women had been to

her, but she managed to put those feelings aside. At that

point, facing elitist snobs was preferable to being around her husband. Every moment between them now felt like an awkward chore. It was hard, painful; she just wanted it to end.

Serenity stopped by her mother-in-law's study to drop off the names of the nobles who were willing to donate to the treasury. The Queen Dowager looked so happy to see her it made her guilty heart feel even worse. "Have a seat," the Dowager told her.

Serenity tried to decline, "I was going to head to the storehouse and see what we can spare for the villages."

"You have been very busy lately. Even busier than my son." Serenity fidgeted nervously.

"I just wanted to make sure things were in order in case-," she stopped herself.

"In case you aren't here?" the Dowager finished. Serenity felt her anxiety spike at being found out. It was this type of thing she'd been trying to avoid as well. How did she tell those around her; those she'd come to care for; those who expected her to rule as Queen, that she was leaving? The Dowager gestured to the seat once more, this time Serenity complied.

"Did he tell you?" Serenity asked.

"He did. It seems as though it's affecting you as much as it's affecting him."

Serenity lowered her head. The truth of those words was not something she wanted to hear. "If you truly are returning soon, I will no longer be able to see you. Can we not speak with each other freely, like a mother and daughter?"

Serenity blinked back the coming tears. "I'm sorry," she said softly.

"You do not need to apologize," the Queen Dowager told her.

"I feel like no matter what I do, someone is going to get hurt because of me," she spoke. "I should be happy- excited even- and I am, but I'm sad and angry too. Why me? Why did I have to go through this? How am I supposed to go back without-," she stopped unable to speak the words. "I think all that, then I feel guilty for thinking that. Then I resent him for making me think that.

"How crazy is that? I'm mad at him because he is so amazing, I don't think I want to leave him," she laughed through her tears. "My family should be my main concern and they are. I will do anything to get back to them. I just wish- I don't even know what I wish," she scoffed. "There's no solution to this. No fix. This is how it is, and I have to just live with it."

"He understands. Even if he can't express that right now; he knows what you struggle with. He has struggles of his own. So, wouldn't it be better to face them together while you can?" The Dowager questioned. Serenity remained quiet, not sure if she had the strength to do what she was suggesting.

"After my husband left this world, I used to sit in our room and just think about all the time I did not spend with him. And I'd curse myself for my stupidity at wasting even a single moment. If you feel even a morsel of what I felt for him, you should not let time go by without filling it with moments you can carry with you." The sincerity in the Dowager's eyes just made her words hit Serenity harder. Everything she said made sense. Even now, she missed Kang-Dae. She missed their talks, his smile, the way he made her feel. She didn't want to give them up, but she would have to. At the very least, she wanted to snatch up every bit of him as she could.

***

That evening Serenity returned to their bedroom. She caught sight of Kang-Dae's crown on its mantle. She looked around, but she didn't see him in the room. A cool wind drew her toward the balcony. Before she could step out onto it, her bewildered gaze fell to the new pallet that was there. There were several pillows resting on top of it and even a thin purple blanket covering it. Kang-Dae was laying out on it staring up at the sky. Curious, she stepped out to join him.

"What's this?" she asked, admiring the new piece of furniture. It looked wonderfully comfortable.

"I had it brought over. I figured we shouldn't have to leave the grounds to lay under the night sky. And now you can continue to pray out here without hurting your knees." Warmth spread through her at his thoughtfulness. Serenity thought back to her conversation with the Dowager. Deciding to take her advice Serenity lay down on the pallet, surprising and delighting Kang-Dae.

"Have you been keeping up with your studies?" he asked.

"Of course."

"Really?" Kang-Dae lifted his finger and did a little 'star writing'.

"What does this mean?"

Serenity lifted her brow. "Well, since you didn't leave space between that line and that dot, I think it means you're a pervert." She said in a semi-serious tone. Kang-Dae thought for a second about how he had 'wrote' his character and blushed when he realized what he'd actually spelled out. Serenity snorted before letting out such joy-filled laughter that he couldn't help joining in. "You're so nasty," she teased as he covered his face with his hands.

"Stop it," he mumbled making her laugh even more.

Having mercy on him she turned her attention back to the sky, writing a message of her own. 'I've missed you.'

She could feel his gaze turn to her, but she couldn't bear to look at him after being so honest. When he repeated her own message back to her in the night sky, her bashfulness turned to delight. The two did some more writing until they grew tired.

They continued to lay next to one another, neither wanting to move. "I think," Serenity began. "we haven't been the best rulers these past few days."

"I think that as well," Kang-Dae agreed. Serenity swallowed contemplating her next words.

"We should go back to fulfilling the people expectancies," she said. Kang-Dae turned sharply to look at her, but he quickly masked his shock.

"I agree," he managed to say. The two fell silent once more. Kang-Dae turned toward her. "I am sorry."

Serenity turned to face him. "Me too. I didn't like that version of us," she stated. "Whatever happens, whenever it happens; I want to go into it together, like we were before." Kang-Dae nodded in agreement.

They watched the sky, both content with their mutual decision. Kang-Dae's hands began to sneak over to her waist. "Stay on your side," she warned.

He let out a groan, pulling a giggle from her.

CHAPTER TEN

Kang-Dae had a little more pep in his step as he
moved through the halls. It seemed things were taking a
turn for the better. There had been word from Kah Mah
inviting them to come and make their partition in person.
He saw this as a good sign. Seeing as it was Serenity's
vision that brought about this good fortune, he wanted her
to know it. He hadn't found her in her study or in the
library where she had been spending so much time lately.

"My King," Yoon called coming towards him. He
bowed to him appropriately. "I was wondering if I might
have a word."

"Later, I need to be at the gate soon and I'm looking
for my wife."

"Oh, I believe she is in the gardens with Jung-Soo,'
he said in a surprisingly helpful tone. Kang-Dae thanked

him and began to head outside. When Yoon followed after him, he did his best not to let his irritation show. "As you know my house's day of establishment is upcoming," Yoon began and Kang-Dae had already started to tune him out. As they walked into the garden, Yoon continued to ramble on about the celebration and how he wanted him to attend. His joy returned seeing Serenity sitting on a bench reading aloud. Jung-Soo was by her side listening intently, something resembling amusement on his normally stoic face. Seeing her so at home, filled him with a longing so deep he didn't notice Yoon had finally stopped talking.

"It is good to see the Queen and Jung-Soo getting along so well. It is a most unusual relationship but a welcome one." Yoon said. Kang-Dae frowned at the term 'unusual' to describe what he felt was a normal friendship. "Not many Queens before her has ever struck up such a bond with a guardsman who was not her own," Yoon continued.

Having no use for the talkative old man, he left him behind and went to retrieve his wife. Her guards followed behind at a distance. As soon as Serenity noticed him, her mouth formed that smile he was so fond of and her eyes brightened, making his heart skip. "Hi," she spoke warmly. He returned the greeting.

"The Queen of Kah Mah has invited us to stay with her for a few days, so we may meet in person."

"Really?" she exclaimed excitedly, shutting her book and standing up. Tickled by her excitement, he took her hand to walk with her. "Also, the shipments from the eastern province have started up once more. I thought you'd want to come with me to receive it."

"Okay," she said eagerly.

"How's the reading coming along?"

"Jung-Soo thinks I need to focus more on my comprehension and less on translating. But if I don't translate, I can't comprehend it," she whined.

"You are right, Jung-Soo is wrong," he said loud enough for the man to hear. Kang-Dae almost tumbled forward when "something" stepped on the heel of his shoe. He looked back and Jung-Soo stood facing forward like he'd had no idea what had happened. Kang-Dae ignored him and kept moving as Serenity fought to keep her laughter in.

As they arrived at the gate, those around them bowed. Representatives from the other provinces were present as well. Kang-Dae had the gates opened. Serenity gasped to see the long line of wagons lining the path. She squeezed his arm and let out a happy noise.

"We will send each of you back home with your share of goods and men to help transport it," Kang-Dae announced. The representatives vocalized their thanks.

"Everyone in our province will know of the Queen's willingness to help the people and the King's generosity," one representative cheered, and the others joined in. Serenity became bashful from the unexpected praise, making Kang-Dae smile. The people were becoming more and more accepting of her which pleased him greatly. He wanted them to see what he saw in her. A dark voice tried to remind him she wouldn't be around much longer, but he refused to acknowledge it. He would keep himself present and not give in to despair of the future.

***

"We waited too long," Jae-Hwa complained. "Whatever was going on between them has resolved."

"It doesn't matter. As rumors of her greatness spread, we will make her flaws and secrets just as well known. Soon, even the King will be unable to ignore it," the conspirator replied.

"How can you be sure words will be enough to sway him?" she asked.

"Words are just one tactic. In war, we use many to ensure victory."

CHAPTER ELEVEN

Serenity yawned putting the book on the history of

Xian back on the shelf. She had finally gotten through it,

though it had been a challenge. Serenity had nothing

against this world's authors, but they did not write for

entertainment. "My Queen, I think you should go rest,"

Gyuri suggested.

"I will, I just wanted to grab one book before I

headed back."

"To what end?" Arezoo questioned.

"I just want something to read before I go to sleep,"

Serenity answered defensively.

"You find time to read when you are in your

chambers with the King?" inquired Arezoo, almost

sounding perplexed at the notion.

"Why is that so surprising?" Serenity asked.

"I just think you wouldn't have the time."

"What do you mean?" questioned Serenity genuinely confused.

"I'm not married my Queen, but I do know what goes on in a marriage bed."

Serenity's brow wrinkled as she tried to comprehend what Arczoo's point was. As soon as she made the connection, she gasped out, "Arezoo!"

"What? It is common for married people, is it not?"

"Is that what you think we're doing every night?" Her slow shrugged made Serenity snort. "Married people don't have to do that every time they're alone," she told her.

"I would," she said it so easily Serenity almost choked on her laughter.

"Nasreen, why is your sister like this?" Serenity joked.

"She has always been this way. No one can figure out why." Arezoo tossed a book at her which she easily dodged.

"I can't with you guys. Let's go," Serenity said.

Once she was back in her room, Serenity dismissed her guard. She moved to take off her heavy dress and stopped. On the table was a vase with a beautiful bouquet. Serenity smiled knowing exactly where they came from. Kang-Dae had been doing things like this a lot in the past few days. Just last week he'd arranged a picnic for them outside the walls, full of her favorite foods. The weather had been perfect and the two fell into natural conversations that lasted hours. Yesterday he took her out horseback riding, claiming she needed to become more comfortable atop the large animal. She'd been nervous the whole time but endured. Now, she at least knew she could ride without falling off. He'd been a patient and kind teacher.

With every gesture, she felt herself becoming more and more enamored with him which delighted and saddened her. She knew they were trying to go on as if they had a future, but she still needed to protect her heart. So, every time she felt herself falling, she thought of her mother and how she must be feeling. The guilt and sadness were enough to keep any delusions she may have at bay.

***

Kang-Dae stared down at the calendar his scholars had presented him with. The date of the blessed moon had been found. A ball of dread formed inside him as he stared at the markings. He had hoped he'd have more time. He'd been taking Jung-Soo's advice to heart, doing his best to show Serenity she had a place there with him. But he didn't think it was enough. Despite his efforts, there was a wall between them; a wall Serenity used to keep him from reaching that special part of herself reserved for those she loved most. If he was unable to break through, the consequences of his failure would haunt him for the rest of his life.

CHAPTER TWELVE

"Katsuo has been pushing further inland," Advisor Min said. The council murmured amongst themselves. Serenity looked over to Kang-Dae who appeared slightly distracted.

"If we send the army, we may stop him from overtaking us," Yu said.

"We can't send out all our forces without knowing exactly where he has positioned his army. We could end up in an ambush." Nasim spoke.

"If we do nothing, he will think us weak. He'll push his boundaries even more," Kyril claimed.

"Has there been any reports that can give us a better idea of where his main forces are?" Serenity asked.

"Not yet, my Queen. So far people have just reported factions of Katsuo's army" Nasim answered.

"If we can map out all the factions, it could give us a possible idea of where he could be," Serenity suggested.

"What do you know of war strategies?" Sun sneered from his position by Yu. His tone shook Kang-Dae out of whatever thought he'd been stuck in.

"General Sun!" The shout brought a tension-filled silence in the room. The general didn't move at first, he stood clenching a fist around the hilt of his sword. He finally moved to the center of the room.

"I think perhaps you are mistaken. You seem to have forgotten who you address," Kang-Dae said in a low voice that made Serenity shudder.

"I meant no offense, my King,"

"Yet I am offended." General Sun went to his knee.

"Apologies, my King."

"Why do you apologize to me?! It is the Queen you should be bending your knee to!"

"It's alright," Serenity chimed in not liking the anger coming from him. "I'm sure he meant no harm." Kang-Dae kept his gaze fixed on Sun. The general wouldn't meet his eye.

"My King?" Serenity called out to him. Kang-Dae finally turned his gaze and sat back against his throne. Serenity let out a relieved sigh. "That'll be all general."

Not wasting a second of his reprieve, Sun quickly rose and returned to his position.

Amir was the first to break the silence bringing them back to the matter they were discussing before.

***

Whatever had been bothering Kang-Dae through the meeting was still bothering him during Serenity's lessons. He was barely present, staring off into space several times. Becoming annoyed with his lack of focus and hating to see him so out of character, Serenity stood and went over to him. Before he could comprehend her movement, she plopped herself down in his lap.

"Wh-wh-what are you doing?" He stammered. It felt good to throw him off balance once in a while, Serenity thought.

"I was trying to work on my grammar, but my teacher doesn't seem to be paying attention." She shifted a bit and Kang-Dae cleared his throat and fidgeted as if he were suddenly very uncomfortable.

She put her paper in his face. "Is this correct?" she asked in Xianian. He swallowed as he glanced down at the paper. He nodded wordlessly. Serenity smiled and grabbed another from her position to begin to write. Kang-Dae was still as a stone as she wrote, paying him no mind. When she was finished, she read what she wrote aloud. Kang-Dae's focus returned, not on her pronunciation or speech, but on her lips. Serenity took notice of where his attention was and sighed dramatically. "Seriously? It's like you don't want me to learn at all." Kang-Dae dropped his gaze and Serenity grinned to see his reddening ears. "Should I go back to my mother-in-law?" She questioned again in Xianian. "At least she knew how to keep the lesson on track," she continued in English. She moved to get up only for him to grab onto her, keeping her in place.

This time, when he looked up at her, it wasn't with the distracted gaze or the anger he had for Sun earlier. It was 100% him. The playfulness and sincerity had returned. She smiled to see it, glad to have him in a better mood. However, her gladness turned to alarm at the realization that he *was* back to his old self and she was currently in his lap. The moment Kang-Dae saw the awareness of her situation hit her, he let loose one of those smiles of his. She tried once more to get up only for his hold to tighten around her. "You have progressed well in your studies," he told her. "So much so, I believe a reward in order."

"I don't need a reward," she squeaked.

"No? Well, what about me? I think the teacher who is responsible for such great progress should share in the spoils as well." Serenity was playing with her hands as her breathing increased.

"What kind of reward?" she asked, eyes shifting. He pretended to contemplate all the while keeping her close, his thumb stroking the small of her back; sending shivers up her spine. His gaze returned to her face, and his playful smile slowly disappeared, replaced with a look Serenity can only describe as hunger. His eyes moved once again to her mouth and Serenity felt like her heart was on the brink of imploding. He moved in slowly, almost as if he were savoring his hunt. Serenity's mind was blank. She couldn't even make up a reason why she shouldn't let this happen. She closed her eyes as his lips met hers. This time there was no hesitation or slow build-up. He kissed her like he was starving for her and planned on devouring her. Her arms wrapped around his neck as she held onto him. His hands moved all over her back and a sound escaped from deep in his throat which stirred something inside her. His kisses deepened, but Serenity pulled away panting in a desperate need to breathe. They stared at one another, breathing in each other's air. Serenity took in his desire filled eyes and reddening lips. This time she was the aggressor as she launched herself at him, joining them together once more. Kang-Dae was caught off guard for a second before he returned her kiss with equal enthusiasm. It was hard to say how long they spent joined together like that. Serenity's mind was barely forming sentences, let alone keeping time. They were both happy to stay in that moment as long as they could. Eventually, they did manage to pull away, resting their heads against one another as they took time to regain their faculties. Kang-Dae was the first to recover. He grinned as he pulled away, taking in her dazed expression. Serenity's face felt hot and it was still hard to focus. Kang-Dae helped her stand. Neither one spoke as he took her hand in his and lead them out of the study, knowing there would be no more work being done in that room that day.

CHAPTER THIRTEEN

Serenity had just come from having tea with the ladies of the court. She of course had drunk her cup last, still being cautious with what she drank and ate. The women wanted to discuss some celebration that they wanted her to host. It had something to do with the Gi family. Just the sound of their name had her wanting to scream out 'no', but she tried to put her biases and extreme dislike of the family aside for the sake of Xian tradition. They spent the time coming up with a reasonable budget. Serenity definitely was not planning on wasting kingdom funds and going all out for that miserable old man and his delusional daughter.

Serenity spotted Jung-Soo on the other side of the pavilion. She called out to him before jogging over holding up her skirts. "I haven't seen you in days," she exclaimed.

"There was some trouble in villages by An Pang river. I took some men to sort it out," he explained.

"You should have told me. I was looking for you."

"All that means to me is that I was lucky enough to be gone when you thought to ask me to participate in some task that I have no interest in." Serenity gave him a dirty look.

"I wanted your help. I wanted to put some protocols in place in specific areas so anyone can take over the shipments," she explained.

"You mean for after you have gone," Jung-Soo completed her sentence. Serenity lowered her head before nodding.

"I can't ask him to help me with things like this," she said softly. "It'll just put us back in a bad place and I don't want that." Jung-Soo was quiet for a second before nodded his understanding.

"Still, I feel offended," Jung-Soo said, suddenly looking wistfully at the sky.

"About what?"

"Do I not merit any special time with the Queen before her departure?" He let out a long sigh. "To think, I thought we were friends." Serenity rolled her eyes and hit him on the arm.

"Are you done being stupid?" She asked playfully. He narrowed his eyes at her, but she wasn't the least bit intimidated. "Come on. I want to get some of it done before dinner."

Kang-Dae watched the two from his spot above them on the walkway. They hadn't noticed him standing there listening to their every word. The darkness in his belly was forming again. Even now, after all they shared, she still would not consider a life with him. She still had every intention of returning home through the unknown to get back to her family. Kang-Dae huffed bitterly. How had he allowed himself to think for a moment she would choose otherwise?

CHAPTER FOURTEEN

Kang-Dae awoke violently out of his sleep, his

nightshirt soaked with cold sweat. His eyes were wild as he

frantically turned to his left. Immense relief filled him

seeing Serenity slumbering peacefully. He reached out to

pull her to him, just to hold her in his arms for a moment to

settle his racing heart but stopped himself. Despite the

urgency he felt, he didn't want to disturb her peace. He

dropped his hand. His heart continued to race as he panted,

trying his best to calm himself, but remnants from his

dream were still in his mind making it impossible. The fear

in his gut was making him nauseous. He glanced over at

Serenity once more. 'She's safe' he told himself over and

over, doing his best to chase that horrible dream away.

Unable to stand the thought of sleep, he rose out of bed.

Grabbing his robe and shoes, he made the long walk to his

study. He sat behind his desk, the silence of the night and

quietness of the palace did nothing to ease the tension he felt. Despite his efforts, he could not shake off his dream. It had been too vivid, too possible. He tried to comfort himself by reminding himself he was not the seer. His dreams didn't come true. But a conversation he'd once had with Serenity when she'd first arrived made him freeze.

Several months earlier

"Are there many seers in your world?" he asked while she wandered around looking at the different weapons and artwork decorating his study. "A lot of them don't even realize it. They think their dreams are just that, dreams. Honestly, that's how they seem until you start to pay attention." She ran her fingers along the ancient mask of his ancestor. "You know even those who aren't technically seers can still have prophetic dreams."

"Really?" he asked skeptically. He inwardly flinched when she poked at the centuries-old cloth painting on the wall.

She nodded. "Not everyone has the gift of prophetic dreaming, but everyone's capable of having prophetic dreams. Sometimes it's dreams of warning, to keep you from doing something that would be bad for you. Or just preparing you for something that's coming. Unfortunately, a lot of people just think they're nightmares and dismiss them. They don't even realize they were given a chance to stop a disaster before it happened."

That sick feeling returned full force. With a shaking hand, he poured himself a cup of wine to settle his nerves. He spent the remainder of the evening at his desk with the lanterns burning through the night.

***

Kang-Dae had been avoiding her all day and she couldn't stand it. When she'd woken up to see his side of the bed empty, she was surprised, thinking maybe he had things to attend to. But as that day became the next, it became clear to her he was once again avoiding her. She thought they'd moved past this. She couldn't figure out what had changed. She shut her book in frustration. According to Jung-Soo, nothing had happened while he was with him. She thought maybe it was something Katsuo related, but then why did it seem like he was specifically taking it out on her? She thought about confronting him, forcing him to explain himself, but she didn't want a fight. The door opened and the subject of her ire walked right in, wearing the same expression of indifference that she'd come to despise. It felt like they were strangers once more. She had hoped he was there to talk and maybe let her know what was bothering him. She watched him with a yearning that was almost embarrassing. How is it possible to miss someone, even if they were in the room?

Kang-Dae stopped right in front of her. "Hi," she said with an uncertain smile hoping he might return it. No such luck.

"My scholars have figured out the day of the next blessed moon." Never had a series of words caused such a competitive state of emotions at once: elation, despair, sadness, anticipation, denial; she was battling every one of them.

"So, what happens now?" she asked her voice low.

"It takes 2 days of travel to get to the lake. We will leave a couple of days before," he said, his tone was flat and emotionless. "Do not worry about the works you have done. I'll make sure they will continue." His detached explanation of what would happen once she was gone was disconcerting. "The people will believe you are visiting relatives for a time. Soon I will break the news that you have grown ill and then I will tell them you have passed." As he continued, like he was just planning an uninteresting business trip, she felt like screaming. "I will make all the preparations."

An uncomfortable silence filled the room. Serenity didn't even know how to respond, not to his attitude, or the fact that she would be going home. "Serenity," he called to her bringing her attention back to him. She was surprised to see that emotionless mask had fallen for a moment.

"What if-," he stopped, his eyes shifting to the floor, as he appeared to struggle to find the right words. "It's possible this may not go the way you think. We still do not know anything about this lake, or what might happen to you if you went in. You could get hurt. Who can say this "doorway" only has one destination? How do you know it will take you back to your home? You could end up in a completely different place- a more dangerous one, and no one to help you."

Serenity tugged anxiously at her dress as a shudder went through her. She honestly hadn't even considered any of those things. So filled with the hope that she could make it home, she never let any other possible outcomes enter her mind. What if she did end up in some terrifying world filled with monsters? What if she wasn't sent to a place where slavery hadn't been abolished? Her blood ran cold at that thought. But this was her best chance, she had to take it.

"I have to try," she stated softly.

"Serenity-,"

"I have to. I have to believe that if I'm meant to go back, I'll make it back."

"And if you don't, and something even worse befalls you?" he pressed. Serenity detected a hint of desperation in his voice.

"It won't," she said confidently. She caught it right before he could hide it away. Pain, regret. It was in his face, his eyes. She wanted to take it away. She took a step toward him only for him to step back.

"I will start making the arrangements." The coldness returned and Serenity could feel her heart clenching. Kang-Dae turned to leave.

"When is it?" she asked stopping him.

"3 weeks," he stated refusing to face her. His answer made her physically ache.

"Are you sure?" she asked doing her best to keep her voice steady.

"Yes." Without another word he left.

Once she was alone, she released a shuddering breath. She began to curse him for making what was already a difficult situation even worse. She wiped her eyes angrily. God help her. She would not leave here this way.

She would not leave him this way. Maybe it was selfish on her part, but she refused to spend what time they had left as drifting strangers.

***

"Has it been arranged?" Yoon asked in a hushed tone being careful despite the secluded spot.

"It's already in place," the conspirator answered.

"How long will we have to wait?"

"It's best if we do this gradually. It will be less suspicious that way." Yoon felt excitement flowing through him at the thought of their plan going into action and what it will mean for him and his family. He couldn't wait to see that false Queen fall and his daughter rise.

CHAPTER FIFTEEN

He felt sick, but also numb. Empty, but full of a dark loathsome feeling. Kang-Dae almost couldn't remember what it was like to not feel uneasy. With every passing day, his trepidation grew and the weight of what was coming was crushing him from the inside out. Food lost all appeal and every moment he was awake was another moment of torment. He didn't know if he could handle it. He continued to work alongside Serenity, but he didn't dare look at her lest his true feelings be revealed. He shielded himself from her with a wall of indifference. He knew her frustration with him was growing, but he dared not speak to her freely, fearing what he might say. Serenity was not making it easy. Amid the anger he knew she was feeling, she still attempted to rectify things between them. She attempted to converse with him, but he would keep his answers short and detached. She would show up in the midst of his work and offer to help, but he would decline. She had even attempted to engage in physical affections. He quickly excused himself, barely able to stop himself from giving in. She'd cornered him one morning before he'd been able to rush out, looking at him with those soft eyes of hers. He could feel himself falling into them. She gave him a sweet smile and offered him a warm good morning.

"Will you have breakfast with me?" she asked innocently enough, though it felt anything but. He made an excuse about having to meet with Yu to talk about the military. She gave a little pout that tugged on his heart. Just as quick as it appeared it was gone, replaced by a sensual curve of her mouth. "Can I tell you goodbye?" He wanted so badly to take her in his arms and let her, but his inner turmoil emerged and he only felt that dark dread inside him when he gazed upon her. He ended up just giving her a terse goodbye before rushing out of the room, ignoring her look of disappointment.

***

They met again that day in the war chamber with the other council members, looking over maps for possible places Katsuo could be keeping his men. Kang-Dae's plan to get the people involved was working gradually. Reports were coming in from across the land. It was simply a matter of figuring out where to strike. His focus was on the task at hand, but other things were pulling on him. Her presence didn't help. It hurt to even look at her. The men talked amongst themselves giving their perspectives on what should be done. In a moment of weakness, he snuck a peek at her and was instantly filled with longing. She dressed simply in a light blue skirt that touched the floor, and a simple white top with light blue trim on the sleeves all held together with a matching blue sash across her waist. Her hair was up, bound with a white ribbon with white hairpins resting in her tight coils. Jung-Soo stood beside her and the two spoke amongst themselves. There was an easement between them he had been missing with her. It made him both envious and angry. He was in constant unrest, yet she could manage to find comfort elsewhere.

"Perhaps if we divert this group to the mountainside, we could force them to the west. The province will hold long enough for us to meet their forces," offered Kyril.

"We still haven't got an accurate count of how many there are," Serenity spoke.

"It will be wise to wait until we have more information before moving," Jung-Soo said agreeing with Serenity.

"Maybe-," Serenity started.

"In war, there are no maybes," Kang-Dae snapped. "We move with certainty when we face death. do you understand?" She stared up at him stunned by his harshness. The room was deadly quiet. Jung-Soo frowned at him with judgment in his eyes effectively shaming him for his actions. He could tell Serenity wanted to speak out, scold him for his harsh words, but she held herself back refusing to make a scene in front of the others. Her thoughtfulness in the middle of her rage just made his guilt worse. Once they were dismissed, he didn't return to the chambers, a cowardly attempt to avoid the storm he caused. Instead, he locked himself in his study along with his pain, guilt, and his regrets.

***

"It's started."

Jae-Hwa felt her happiness grow. "Truly. Has he cast her aside?"

"Patience, it'll take a bit more to push him that far but judging from his actions today I would say our plan is moving along."

Jae-Hwa was surprised. "I did not think to see progress so soon. I thought her hold on him would cause more of a fight."

Yoon's eyes shifted. "Well, you never know the power of suggestion until it is used," he said vaguely. Jae-Hwa regarded him carefully. He was avoiding her gaze. Was he not telling her something? She dismissed the thought. Whatever it was, it must have been in her best interest and she did not need to know. She was fine with that as long they achieved their goal. If this were to work, all she would be that much closer to becoming the Queen she was always meant to be.

CHAPTER SIXTEEN

Kang-Dae would not sleep tonight, he knew that.

He was not going to try. There was nothing in this world that could fill him with enough ease to allow him the luxury of sleep. Every hour of this day had been tortuous, worse than he could have imagined. He'd been unable to focus or control his conflicting emotions and had unwittingly directed his frustration at Serenity. That had only made things worse in his already restless mind. He was prepared to spend the rest of the night right there in his study, but the need to at least check on Serenity was far too great. He just wanted to make sure she was alright, then he could return. As late as it was, he knew she would be sleeping.

He opened the door to their chambers as quietly as he could. The room was shrouded in darkness. Kang-Dae shut the door carefully not wanting to wake her. As he moved toward the bed, he saw from the corner of his eye that the balcony doors were wide open. He turned slowly until his heart dropped at the sight of Serenity on the balcony. She was only dressed in her night clothes while she stared up at the sky.

Serenity hadn't heard him come in. She had purposely turned out all the lights, so he would feel safe enough to enter. She'd been out there for a while praying to God for strength, patience, and understanding. Once her temper had cooled, she took the time to try and understand what Kang-Dae was going through. He was clearly in pain. Although it would be easy to just dismiss his behavior as unacceptable and blow up at him, she wanted to ease his hurt- not add to it. "Come inside," Kang-Dae's voice had the same harshness as earlier. 'On the other hand,' she thought to herself.

"Now." She tensed up as her irritation rose once more. Serenity took a long slow breath and counted to three before releasing it. Turning to face him, she became even more annoyed at the anger it displayed. *'Like he had the right to be mad right now,'* she thought.

"Is that all you have to say to me?" she demanded starting to care less and less as to why he was behaving this way.

"Come inside," he repeated.

"No." He had the nerve to reach for her as if he meant to force her inside. She quickly sidestepped him. "I expected something more on the lines of, 'I'm sorry, forgive me," she stated, almost daring him to say something different. He only moved to grab her again and once again she avoided him.

"Stop it. I'm sick of this! I'm done trying to make things easier for you. You clearly would rather sulk and mope, and treat me like garbage than act like a damn grown-up and face this together."

"Together!" He blustered making her jump. "That word should taste bitter on your tongue. How dare you speak about unity when you relish the day you'll be free from me."

"That is not true," Serenity denied clenching her fist at her sides.

"No? You said over and over how important it was for you to leave- leave this palace, this land... me," his voice cracked over the word. "You made it clear I was never in your heart the way you were in mine." His confession tore at her in her anger began to die down. "You plan to just leave me behind and continue your better life in a better land. Maybe you'll find a better man. Someone worth your affections, someone you couldn't bear to say goodbye to no matter the circumstance." Tears sprang to her eyes as he poured out his feelings. "I was the fool. I thought if you felt even a tiny bit of what I feel for you it might be difficult for you to even consider leaving, but clearly, it's easy for you to dismiss me, us, what we meant to one another."

"Easy? Do you think any of this is easy for me? This is the single most horrible and hardest thing I've ever had to do." He let out a scoff and folded his arms disbelieving. "I essentially had to decide who's suffering I could live with more: theirs or yours. At least you'll know I'm safe. I won't be alone. I'll be with the people that love me. My family doesn't have that reassurance. Every moment of happiness I could find here would be tainted with the knowledge that I got it through their pain."

"What about my pain? Does it not matter to you?" Kang-Dae shot back.

"I just wanted to have your memory with me," she tried to explain, her fury turning to sorrow at every word from him.

"Is that what you think I need, memories of someone who tossed me aside, cast aside all we had? You think the memory of your smile, your kiss, your heart will be a comfort to me. You just made my hell that much worse."

Serenity turned away unable to stomach the pain in his eyes. "I'm sorry," she cried.

"What does your sorry do for me? Can I hold it in my arms? Talk to it, feel the warmth of its comfort? You have nothing to offer me but an empty confession and pain," he raged on.

Serenity whirled back around, facing him, her eyes red. "Everything you feel, I feel it too. It feels like I'm sick, and it's just getting worse. I walk around here smiling and laughing and working my way through it, but inside I feel like I'm dying, knowing the pain I'll cause when I leave. But if I stay, I'll feel like I'm dying too. Either way, there's going to be pain. But that's the burden I have to bear. It's my hell to endure because I have to go home. I have to." Kang-Dae stood stiffly not saying anything. He appeared as if he hadn't heard her until she saw his face fall.

"I'm sorry," he said in Xianian, his voice cracking. "I'm so sorry." The anguish in his tone just made her heartbreak more. She rushed over to him wiping at his tears before they could fall.

"It's okay. It's okay," soothed Serenity.

"I'm sorry."

"You don't have to be sorry. None of this is your fault," she tried to comfort him.

"No Serenity I-," she silenced him with a kiss, the taste of her tears on their lips. She pulled away for a second staring into his haunted brown eyes before kissing him again.

'Stop her. Stop this,' Kang-Dae's head demanded. His hands were fisted at his sides, clenching so tightly his nails almost drew blood. He knew he should pull away, but he couldn't bring himself to. Pulling away was returning to that darkening abyss of grief and turmoil. Pulling away would be accepting what was going to transpire and what that would mean for her, for him, and for the future. The feel of her soft lips on his was more than a reprieve, it was paradise. How could one trade paradise for hell? He was not that strong. In a last-ditch effort to contain himself, he placed his hands on her shoulders with the intent of pushing her away. But before he could, Serenity's hands were suddenly in his hair pulling him down deeper into her kiss, and he was lost. All the longing, the need, the desire he had for her- all that he purposely attempted to hold back over the course of several days had been unleashed. He couldn't get enough. He kissed her desperately as if she would disappear at any moment. At some point, her knees went weak and he held her up.

Serenity wondered if this is what the women in romance books meant when they claimed they saw stars. Even though they were under the night sky, she knew the stars she was seeing were unrelated. He was kissing her senseless. Thoughts no longer processed. Up, down, none of it mattered at that moment. There was nothing, nothing but them. She was suddenly weightless, as her feet left the ground. She felt the softness of the pallet on her back. The intensity in his gaze was almost too much. He kissed her softly this time, letting his lips linger. He started laying kisses down her cheek, to her throat and collarbone. When his lips dipped even lower to the valley between her breasts, she sucked in a breath. He raised his eyes to meet hers, watching her as he placed gentle wet kisses right at the swell of her breast. She couldn't get enough air even though she was outside. Her hands clutched at the padding beneath her as he trailed back up to her throat finding the perfect spot nibbling on it so deliciously, she let out a moan. The sound only spurred him on as he moved to do the same thing on the other side. She began to wonder why she had yet to stop him. This would only make things worse.

She brought his face back to hers as they stared into each other's eyes, hearts, souls. Serenity hesitated. If she allowed this, if they crossed this line, she knew in her heart she could only survive one night. Just tonight, just this one night to express everything they needed to without the complexity of words. Her hands reached out to grab his shirt, intending to remove it when he suddenly pulled away. Serenity stared up at him confused by his actions. Kang-Dae gently shook his head, making her frown. She was about to question him when he was on her once more, silencing her with his mouth. His hands roamed all over, causing her stomach to tighten. She was starting to feel overwhelmed by it all. Every time she thought it was becoming too much, he'd pull away allowing her to breathe, just for a second, taking the chance to kiss whatever parts of her he could reach. Once she caught her breath, he returned to her to do it all over again. Vaguely, she wondered why he wouldn't go further. With the way he was making her feel, she'd let him do whatever he wanted but he never stopped kissing her and making her body ache for more of his touch. His hands moved all over her, touching parts of her no one ever had before. When his hand grazed her thigh, she almost died on the spot. It could've been seconds, minutes, or hours before his kisses started to slow; becoming gentler, lingering ever so sweetly. He slowly lifted his head to stare into her eyes. "saranghae," he whispered in her ear, placing a soft kiss on her pulse. She didn't recognize the word, but she was far too dazed to comprehend anything at the moment. Eventually, he gathered her in his arms holding her close to him. Warm, safe, loved. Serenity felt it all in his embrace as she listened to the beating of his heart. In that moment she could feel it, whether she admitted it or not, this man had her heart. 'Why does this feel like home,' was her last thought before she drifted to sleep.

CHAPTER SEVENTEEN

Serenity woke up in their bed under the blanket with strong arms around her. She smiled to herself as she realized he must have carried her over at some time during the night. She looked up and her heart skipped seeing Kang-Dae watching her, his grin making her heart dance. "Morning," she said shyly in Xianian.

"Morning," he replied, his voice sounding deeper than normal, or maybe that was just her. "Sleep well?" he asked. She nodded.

"You?" He nodded as well. Serenity wasn't exactly sure what to say at a moment like this. What do you say after a night like that? "You-," she began. He raised his eyebrow. "You're on my side," she finished suddenly. Kang-Dae looked puzzled until understanding hit him and he let out the sexiest laugh she ever heard. Suddenly, she was rolling. When the room stopped spinning, he was staring down at her and she was beneath him.

"Now you're on my side." Serenity giggled. He kissed her softly. He was about to do it a second time.

"We have to get up," She told him. She did her best not to laugh when he pouted. "The sun's pretty high. I think we overslept," she explained. He let out a disappointed sigh.

"Can we at least have breakfast together?" She smiled and nodded. After kissing her above her eye, he finally released her. He picked up his robe. "I'll be back," he said before walking out of the room. Once alone, Serenity covered her face with her hand still reeling over the events of last night. Even though they didn't go beyond kissing, it was still a wonderfully intimate experience that she was glad she could share with him. It would be a memory she would cherish for the rest of her life.

***

Amoli was sewing up a rip in the Queen's dress. Across from her, the Queen sat at the table, writing. The Queen had asked for her help in writing personal letters to the King so she could comfort him even when she was gone. Amoli didn't like to think about her Queen and friend leaving. It filled her with such sadness to know that the country was not only losing such a fine queen, but she was also losing her most cherished friend. A part of her understood her Queen's desire to return to the land of her birth. Amoli missed her family as well. They had sent her off, hoping she would have a better life in the capital, not wanting her to be stuck in their small village only hoping to become a bride and nothing more. She missed them every day. But in the end, they knew she was safe, and she knew the same. It was different for her Queen and she understood that, but it didn't stop her from wanting her to stay. She'd seen the influence she'd had, not just on the King, but the

131

people as well. Her Queen may not have noticed, but Amoli did. Her desire to help the people and personally go out to make sure they had what they needed had inspired some of the nobles. Families Amoli had never even seen lift a finger without the help of a servant, were making the effort to go out into the cities and villages to give aid where they could. Amoli had thought more than once, that perhaps fate had brought her here for a purpose, one beyond what her Queen could see.

"Do you need help, my Queen?" Amoli asked, realizing the Queen had not asked for a translation in a while. She looked to be struggling to find the right words.

"No, it's fine. I can figure it out. Besides, this one is for you, so I don't want you to see it yet." Amoli stopped in the middle of her stitch.

"For me?"

"Yeah, just in case you miss me." Amoli's eyes welled up with emotion.

"I will," she told her. "I will miss you." The Queen looked up from her writing and gave her a warm smile.

"I'll miss you, too." The Queen stood and walked over to her. Amoli's eyes widened when she hugged her. Amoli was too dumbstruck to react at first. The Queen pulled away. "Okay that's enough of that, you're not going to make me cry today," she declared with a sniff. The Queen went back to her writing. Amoli went back to sewing, in her mind she wished her Queen would never leave.

CHAPTER EIGHTEEN

Jung-Soo was watching the soldiers train. They wielded their swords decently, but Jung-Soo expected better. On the brink of war, there could be no weaknesses. He had volunteered to check on the forces at their largest fort closest to the city. He told himself he had come to make sure their forces would be ready once the war finally began. He wanted to believe he came for selfless reasons, but the truth was he needed the time away. The royal couple was on better terms. It was apparent as soon as he saw them. As relieved as he was that they were doing better, it didn't lessen the longing he had. Every not so secret look between them, the small touches they gave one another reflexively- even watching them agree with one another was becoming hard to see. He just needed to take a few days to himself to get his head clear and purge these useless and burdening feelings. The sound of a gong hit his ears. Down below in the courtyard, two men were screaming and aggressively pushing each other. Jung-Soo headed down to see what was going on.

"You dare disrespect our Queen like that?" A young recruit shouted.

"She never should have been Queen in the first place. She is a foreigner who has bewitched our King." The younger man shoved the older one so hard he stumbled. Bellowing out a cry, the older soldier raised his practice sword and charged at the recruit only to face plant in the dirt. Jung-Soo moved his foot back as he looked down on the older soldier.

"You should be training, not fighting," he chastised. The embarrassed soldier jumped to his feet ready to attack the one who'd caused his fall, but he faltered when he saw Jung-Soo. Lowering his hand in respect, he apologized.

"Sorry sir, it will not happen again."

"Since you have the time to talk politics, I'm sure your swordplay is more than efficient?" Jung-Soo questioned.

"Y-yes, sir," the soldier stuttered, refusing to meet Jung-Soo's gaze.

"Show me."

"Sir?"

"Attack me," Jung-Soo said firmly, still not raising his voice. The man's eyes widened. He tried to decline, bowing down to Jung-Soo claiming he could never harm a superior officer, but Jung-Soo would not let up.

"This superior officer is giving you an order. Are you not willing to obey?" he chided. The soldier weighed his options. He took in Jung-Soo's empty hands and returned his gaze to his face still trying to determine if he was serious. Deciding he meant what he said, he finally took his sword in hand. He stood without moving for a long while, clearly uncomfortable.

"Attack," Jung-Soo goaded. The man let out a yell before charging at him. Jung-Soo avoided him easily and put his foot out, effectively sending him face down in the dirt once again. This time when the man got up his lip was bleeding. The soldier spit blood into the dirt before pulling himself up. His anxiety gave way to anger. He took his sword in hand again, but instead of charging he waited, thinking up his best course of action. He circled Jung-Soo slowly, purposely. Jung-Soo remained still not even following him with his eyes. Heavy footsteps from behind him told him to move. As soon as he did, the soldier almost ran past him, but Jung-Soo caught him by the back of his shirt. Yanking it hard it caused the soldier to fall backward, his head bouncing on the ground. Jung-Soo put his foot on his chest, leaning all his weight onto it. The man began to wheeze. He tried to push Jung-Soo off, but he wouldn't budge.

"Next time, focus more on your skills and less on useless gossip." Nodding frantically the soldier was trying desperately to catch his breath. Jung-Soo held his position a few more seconds before finally releasing him. He stared at the soldier with a cold glare as he scurried away, leaving his dignity behind. It wasn't until he was gone that Jung-Soo noticed that a crowd had formed and had watched the whole thing. One look from Jung-Soo had them all scrambling to get back to training.

As Jung-Soo left the courtyard, he silently reprimanded himself. He probably should have handled that better. There were always going to be ignorant men who believed the worst of others- even their rulers, no matter what. He'd heard more than a few unkind words spoken about Kang-Dae over the years, but he never took it to heart. But hearing ill words being spoken of Serenity stirred up something in him and he felt a need to defend her. That voice returned, taunting him, letting him know that even away from the palace she was still affecting him.

CHAPTER NINETEEN

Serenity was being chased. No matter how fast she,

ran she couldn't lose the dark shadow coming after her.

She refused to look back, too fearful to even gaze at the

ominous figure. She raced towards her old home where she

had grown up. The closer she got to the house the slower

she seemed to go, and she could feel that malevolent

shadow getting closer. She let out a whimper as she

struggled to get her legs to move faster. The shadow was

almost upon her now. Her heart pounded as the dark

feeling at her back increased. Just when she was sure that

horrible darkness would catch her, a hole opened up in

front of her. She stumbled into it before she could stop

herself, falling into the unknown. But as quickly as she fell,

she landed even faster on something soft. Looking around

she was surprised to see she was sitting atop a large pile of

something purple. Reaching to investigate what she had

landed in, her attention was drawn up. A wisp of the

darkness lingered over the edge, waiting.

Serenity opened her eyes, chasing away any lingering feelings of sleep. The darkness in the room did nothing to calm her already racing heart. The memories of that awful darkness were still fresh in her mind. As she began to waken a bit more, she registered Kang-Dae's arms around her. She focused on the warm feeling of being in his embrace, allowing him to chase away her fears even in his sleep. Despite that, she was tempted to wake him and share her dream, but she stopped herself. 'What if he took it as a bad omen?' Serenity did not want to give him any more reason to stop her from returning home. She lay there trying to convince herself the dream wasn't a warning. It couldn't be. She tried to hold on to the fact that in the dream she had been fine. She had managed to avoid the shadow in the end. Still, the most chilling and worrying part of the whole thing was the fact that she had never made it back home.

***

Kang-Dae was in a mood, anyone who crossed his path could tell. His counsel avoided him, and the servants were quick to do their tasks and run away. He rubbed at his throbbing head. He was sure these headaches were being brought on by stress as they were occurring regularly now. Between Serenity's anticipated departure, Katsuo's boundary-crossing and feeding a nation, he was feeling overwhelmed. On the surface, Serenity and he were the epitome of a happy couple. Though the moments they shared were genuine, the looming presence of what was to come was always there, making every single second they spent together bittersweet. He continued to enjoy his time with her, but it took effort to act as though everything was fine. For her sake, he tried to hide all the things keeping him up at night. Often, he found himself lying awake watching her wishing that things could be different. He felt like dropping to his knees before her every time he looked into her eyes.

Serenity unceremoniously burst into his study and preceded to drag him out of his chair. "I still have more to do," he tried to protest, but she would not hear it.

"You are done. You're tired and you're hurting," she said in Xianian to emphasize her seriousness, leaving him no room to argue. He allowed her to pull him out of the room. Every step was like a knife in his head. The steady pounding only growing worse. Serenity led them to their chambers. She sat him on the daybed by the window. Grabbing the pillow in her hands, she sat and placed it in her lap while ordering him to lie down. Obediently, he complied placing his head on the pillow. Immediately, she began rubbing at his temples in an attempt to ease away his tension. The tension in him slowly dissipated as the pain begin to dull. He wanted to sigh out in relief.

"You can't do this. No more working yourself so hard. You'll work yourself to death." To him, the notion seemed almost preferable. "You have to take care of yourself. Everyone needs you strong," she told him. He let out a low sound of agreement. The minutes passed as they sat there silently until Serenity started humming. The sound was so beautiful and melodic, he almost immediately began to fall asleep. He said something to her in Xianian that he couldn't stop himself from saying.

"I don't know what that means," she said.

"Study," was all that he said, earning him a light pinch. With a small smile, he turned into her, wanting-needing to be as close as possible. He needed her kindness and warmth, more than ever to face what was ahead.

CHAPTER TWENTY

Jung-Soo had returned from the fort only after a couple of days. He claimed it was because he wanted to report back as soon as possible, but Kang-Dae knew the real reason. The time was almost upon them, he did not want to miss it. "Has everything been arranged?" Jung-Soo asked in his usual nonchalant way.

"We will leave in two days. The council has been informed she will be visiting relatives for a short time," Kang-Dae answered keeping his voice neutral despite the sick feeling he had inside.

"Is that all?" Jung-Soo pushed. The question 'will you be alright' was hanging in the air. Kang-Dae stared ahead. "My feelings will be irrelevant," he said finally, causing Jung-Soo to look at him. His voice was heavy, filled with obvious grief, but there was still something else underneath- something Jung-Soo had yet to place. The duo sat in contemplating silence, each dealing with their own woes, preparing for what was to come. To think, just a few months ago their thoughts were only on the kingdom's plights, how they longed to go back to such a simple time.

***

Serenity sipped her tea as she tried to keep her emotions in check. Her mother-in-law had invited her for one last meeting before her departure. The mood was somber and there were hardly any words spoken, but just being in her company was comforting. Her mother-in-law didn't pry or force the conversation out of her. When they did talk, it was about mundane things. It helped keep her heavy heart from overwhelming her. However, she knew she couldn't leave without telling the woman what her support meant to her. "Thank you," she said suddenly. The Queen Dowager stopped in the middle of bringing her cup to her lips. Really wanting her to hear her, Serenity spoke Xianian.

"I am grateful for all the kindness you have shown me and to have met you. I could not have asked for a more wonderful mother-in-law." The Queen Dowager slowly put her cup down. She made her way over to Serenity. Taking Serenity's hand in hers, she used the other to cradle her face. "You are the most wonderful daughter a mother could ever hope for. Even if it was for a short while, I'm glad to have had you as a part of my family."

The Dowager embraced her, and Serenity returned the hold eagerly as she did her best to hold back her tears. Why did it feel like she was leaving one family for another?

That night Serenity barely slept, spending most of the night watching Kang-Dae. She thought of every moment they'd had together, how they'd grown from their first meeting. From the first day, he'd been her protector, a light in the midst of fear and darkness. Serenity never could have anticipated falling so hard for him back then. Past Serenity would have been scolding her for her stupidity and she couldn't blame her. The way her heart ached at the thought of saying goodbye now, only proved she'd been correct in her assumption that it would make things much harder for her. Knowing that, she felt she couldn't make herself regret it, not when he'd also brought her so much joy. She softly touched his hair taking a strand behind his ear, allowing her thumb to linger on his cheek. Leave it to her to find the one in an impossible land. 'God please give me the strength. Give him peace in his heart and keep him safe. Keep them all safe,' she prayed.

Unbeknownst to Serenity, Kang-Dae was wide awake, enjoying her little ministrations physically but dying inside. The knot in his stomach was so big it hurt. 'Could he go through with this?' The urge to open his eyes and beg her to stay filled him for the millionth time, but he held back. She'd made herself clear. She would never willingly make Xian her home. He was in no way ready for what was to come, but he would have to endure it and face the consequences.

***

The council and court watched as the King and Queen prepared to depart along with Jung-Soo and the Queen's handmaiden. Satori thought it was strange that she did not bring her guard. Though he found a lot strange with the whole situation. Satori was questioning the so-called existence of these relatives he'd never heard of before. They still hadn't been told from what land she'd hailed from. He took a glance at advisor Min, who was staring at the King oddly. Was it disappointment? Something was going on. The man had never explained the bruising on his face once he reemerged after claiming to be ill. The King was hiding things. Ever since that woman arrived, he not only lost his power, he'd lost the King's ear and now the right to be involved. It would be best if she didn't return. Perhaps he would make that prayer when he visited the temple. If gods be good, they would grant his wish.

Kang-Dae helped Serenity on up on her horse. They did not bring a carriage, wanting to be inconspicuous as possible. That was part of his excuse for not bringing any of their guards. No one could know about what they planned. The only ones he allowed were already in the know about Serenity's origins. His mother had wanted to go with them, but he denied her. He still needed someone he trusted to maintain things in his absence. He didn't want anyone trying anything. She'd been disappointed but understanding. The two women had shared an emotional goodbye that he had to look away from. His guilt was eating up at him once more. Serenity wanted to give her guard a proper farewell, but without explaining to them what was going on, it was impossible. Instead, she told them she would see them soon. He saw how hard it was for her to pretend she would return. She'd still hugged each of them to their shock. Arezoo had been the most uncomfortable. Kang-Dae thought maybe she was suspecting something. He pushed for Serenity to leave just in case. Serenity glanced around the palace for the final time, the place that had started to feel like home to her. She would miss the views, the peace, the quietness of it all. The gates opened, forcing herself to look ahead she trotted behind her husband leaving behind her Queenly title.

CHAPTER TWENTY-ONE

The first day was a bit light, filled with conversation and a little joking between her, Jung-Soo, and Amoli; though sometimes the younger woman became too flustered to speak. Kang-Dae did not join in as much. His solemn demeanor wasn't surprising, but she hoped they could pretend a little, so her final days wouldn't be so sad.

When they had stopped for the night, he held her so tight it was uncomfortable. Butut she didn't complain because she was feeling the same desperation he was. Instead of getting him to loosen his grip, she returned it just as fiercely. They didn't speak, both knowing nothing could be said.

***

Serenity dreamt she was wandering around an empty house. She kept calling out for her mother and father, but no one answered. As she searched each room looking for traces of anyone, pictures began to line the walls. She didn't pay attention to them at first, too concerned with finding her family. As she ran frantically downstairs shouting for her mother, she came to a stop. On the mantle of the fireplace was a wedding picture. Only instead of her parents, it was of her and Kang-Dae. She was wearing a modern white wedding dress while he wore the same red wedding attire he had when they were married. She picked up the picture, careful not to knock down the red vase that was housing a single purple flower next to it. She held the picture as she continued searching for her family. More and more pictures kept appearing- only they weren't pictures of her family, but people from Xian. She passed a photo of the Queen Dowager with Serenity as a young child sitting in her lap. In another, Amoli was wearing a beautiful gold sari. Her hair was incredibly long, almost flowing to her knees. Serenity was hugging her from the side, dressed in her dark green prom *dress smiling brightly for the camera. A photo of a stone-faced Jung-Soo in front of a police station while Serenity gave the bunny ears sign behind his back caught her attention. It was an exact copy of a picture she'd taken with her brother after he graduated from the police academy. Serenity passed the window, not even noticing that outside were the palace grounds. Serenity began to call out to her family louder. She was home, but where was everyone? Why was she alone?*

The next day the mood was positively somber. No one joked or even spoke. Serenity spent most of the time trying to hold back her tears. She kept telling herself she would feel better when she saw her family. She had to believe that the pain wouldn't be too much once she was back with them, but with the way she was feeling, she knew that wouldn't be the case. Her dream from last night was also on her mind. She couldn't figure out what it could mean. Was it telling her she was unconsciously replacing her family with those around her? Was it just voicing her deep fears of choosing between them? The empty house had put her on edge. Why was her family not there?

Kang-Dae felt sick, filled with a poisonous feeling of dread that only grew as the day wore on. There was no amount of preparation or pre-thought he could do that would get him ready for what was to take place. He could only think about how to live with it, for her sake and those depending on him.

"Can we stop for a moment?" Serenity's sudden question brought everyone out of their personal introspective. Without really waiting for confirmation, Serenity dismounted on her own with some difficulty, not waiting for any help. She walked off into the woods. Kang-Dae looked to Jung-Soo who just gave a nod.

Kang-Dae dismounted and followed her, leaving the other two on the road. He found her quickly standing among the trees. When he got closer to her, he thought she was speaking to herself, but then he realized she was praying. "Give me strength. Please settle my heart. Grant me enough peace just to make it." Kang-Dae felt a pang in his heart listening to her pleading words. Unable to stop himself he wrapped his arms around her waist hugging her to his chest. She paused in the middle of her prayer and relaxed against him. They stood silently trying to hold on to the moment, neither of them wanting to be the first to let go. When he felt the tears fall on his sleeve, he closed his eyes trying to keep his own at bay. The question he'd been holding back- the one he never asked because deep down he already knew the answer, was on his tongue. A last-ditch effort to spare them both this pain. "Serenity," he spoke. He felt her stiffen in his arms. Still, he opened his mouth to continue, but she spun around and kissed him hard. He was momentarily stunned by the intensity of it. His fingers dug into her back as he allowed her to pour her heart out with her kiss. When she pulled back slightly out of breath, he could see the resolve in her eyes. He put his question back in his heart. He leaned forward and pressed his lips to her head. 'So be it.'

***

The moon shined above, providing a little light in the darkness. It was hard to see, but they could not stop. Tonight, was her chance. The butterflies in her stomach had been plaguing her for the past hour. She was almost there; she was almost home. The memory of the shadow from her dream had come into her mind putting a trickle of fear inside her. She forced the feeling away. She was going home, she had to believe that. "Here." Kang-Dae's voice made her heart jump.

The group dismounted and led the horses into the trees. Serenity saw the lake, she felt her excitement rising and falling like a rollercoaster. She approached the lake slowly. She could feel that panic beginning to stir whenever she was near bodies of water, but she kept willing it away. She stared up at the moon. It didn't seem any different. The crescent moon was partly obscured by dark clouds. She took in a deep breath. Turning back to those that accompanied her, her eyes met Amoli's first. She hugged her friend tightly.

"Thank you," she whispered. She heard Amoli sniffle in her ear as she clung to her.

"Be safe, My Queen," Amoli said, voice cracking.

Jung-Soo was next. Despite his stiff posture, she hugged him to her. He stood rigidly before slowly returning her embrace. "I'll miss you," she told him. He didn't respond but she never expected him to. Instead, his hold tightened. She smiled, hugging him just as tightly before he finally released her.

As she approached Kang-Dae, he wouldn't look at her, keeping his gaze firmly on the ground. She had to raise his eyes to meet hers. The pain she saw in them made her falter. Whatever she wanted to say to him didn't seem enough... nothing did. She decided one last kiss would have to do. A last-minute thought came to her and she reached for her necklace, carefully removing it and placing it in his hands.

"I cannot-"

"If it wasn't for this, I never would've met you. Keep it, so you have something to remember me by." Kang-Dae shut his eyes tightly. "I really loved being your Queen," she said with a quiver. She hugged him so tightly she could feel his heart racing. She forced herself to let go, knowing if she didn't, she never would.

Her feelings bounced between excitement, dread, happiness, and sorrow with every step toward the lake. She had no idea what she was doing, but she figured the water, with the help of the moon, would do all the work like before.

The first step into the cold water made her want to jump back, but she pressed on. The more she was submerged the more her heart pounded in her ears. Nothing happened. She decided to swim out into the middle and wait for the same pull that had brought her here. She waited for a few moments, but nothing happened. Maybe she hadn't found the right place. She took a breath and dove. The murkiness of the water and the darkness of the night made it impossible to see but she kept swimming, desperate to find the same whirlpool that had brought her here. She swam to her left, right, to the front, to the side- but nothing was happening. She felt the cold hands of despair grip her heart. Her dream was no longer in the back of her mind, but screaming at her. She dived again and again and again barely coming up for air. She could hear the concerned voices of Kang-Dae and Jung-Soo, but she ignored them. Her lungs began to burn, but she dared not come up- not until she found her way home. As she felt herself become lightheaded something pulled her. Hope began to fill her, believing she'd found it. But when she reached the surface in Kang-Dae's arms, her heart fell.

"What are you doing? I just have to keep trying!" she cried out desperately.

"You are going to kill yourself!" he argued back. She moved to go under once more, but he stopped her. She pushed him.

"Stop! It'll work. I know it will!" she tried once more to go under, but Kang-Dae had enough and dragged her to shore. She fought, begged, and screamed. Jung-Soo had to help pull her out. "Let me go!" she shrieked. "I'm going to miss it! The sun will be up soon. I have to go back!" Neither man would release her. She struggled against them, cursing at them, hitting them. Doing everything she could to try to get back in.

Eventually, Jung-Soo was the one to pin her down. "Serenity!" he shouted silencing her. Desperate eyes stared up at him. "Sometimes doors only open one way."

The words were like a knife in her heart. She shook her head. "No!" She cried out, not wanting to believe it. "It'll work. It has to," she said, but everyone could hear the uncertainty in her voice. She let out a sob. "Please, please let me try again," she begged them. Jung-Soo released her so Kang-Dae could take her in his arms. "I have to try again," she kept repeating over and over into his chest. Kang-Dae held her as her body convulsed with sobs. The scream she released broke his heart in two. "I'm sorry. I'm so sorry," he whispered into her in Xianian, as she cried out in despair.

CHAPTER TWENTY-TWO

Kang-Dae accepted the tray of food, not allowing the servant in the room. He set it down on the table, grabbed the rice, and took it over to the bed where Serenity lay and had been laying for over two weeks. The only time she got up was to relieve herself and when Kang-Dae would take her to bathe- with Amoli's help. She didn't want to see or be around anyone. She barely acknowledged his presence. She'd become a shell of her former self, from the moment they brought her back to the palace. She didn't speak or show any kind of emotion. She was broken. Seeing her this way was killing him. He was doing his best to be there for her, to keep her healthy so when she did find her way back to the surface he would be there. When her attempts at going home had failed, he vowed to do whatever he could to make this place a home for her. Once they got through this, when she returned to herself, he would spend his life and all his efforts making her happy.

Kang-Dae helped her sit up. She didn't look at him at all. She hadn't acknowledged him or anyone since her return. He took his time feeding her. She took small bites, not showing any indication of whether she liked it or not. It was just the task her body did automatically. He fed her until she wouldn't accept any more. As usual, it wasn't much. He sometimes got so preoccupied with making sure she was fed, he would skip his own meals. He watched her at all times, hardly ever getting any sleep himself. She drank a few sips of water before laying back down. He put the bowl and cup away. He had his guard turn away anyone who came looking for them, not caring to be bothered with anyone or anything. He refused to leave her side. His wife was his priority at the moment. He wasn't going to push her to recover. He knew she was in mourning. She was grieving the loss of her family, her old life, and all her hopes that she would return one day. But he would help her through it no matter how long it took. He had failed her, it was only right he take the responsibility.

***

"This won't do. It won't work if this keeps up," Yoon said. He had been disappointed when the King arrived back with the Queen, thinking her absence could only help their plan. They decided to continue, but hit a wrinkle when the King disappeared into their chamber and refused to come out. The King's captain gave some excuse about the Queen becoming ill on the journey and having to return.

"We can only wait. This can't last much longer. Once they reappear, we will double our efforts. Now more than ever it's important we remove her. She's an unneeded distraction and a burden on him." His co-conspirator spoke. Yoon nodded in full agreement.

***

Serenity didn't feel alive. She knew she wasn't dead, but she couldn't feel anything. She was completely numb. But it was much better than the gut-wrenching agony she had felt at the lake. She just wanted to stay this way until that horrible grief went away. Her eyes threatened to well up again as she thought on it, but she shut them defiantly.

"Serenity?" She heard Kang-Dae call to her, but she didn't answer- she couldn't. She still couldn't bring herself to speak to him or anyone, knowing it would just cause her to breakdown again. If she allowed herself to feel all that she lost, she was terrified of what she might do to herself. The idea of doing anything to stop the pain was prickling in the back of her mind and she kept it at bay by choosing not to feel it all. She didn't know how long she would, or could, continue living like this.

CHAPTER TWENTY-THREE

Jung-Soo walked with purpose. He held back for days, hoping things would get better. But every time he saw Kang-Dae as he practically carried Serenity to the bath, he was looking more and more worn. There were dark circles under his eyes and his skin looked to be losing its hue. He decided if Kang-Dae wouldn't put a stop to this he would.

The guard posted outside the room moved to bar his entry. "The King ordered-," the guard began.

"Are you going to stop me?" Jung-Soo interrupted, stepping up to the guard whose eyes began to shift nervously. Thinking better of it, he stepped away and Jung-Soo went inside.

Kang-Dae looked like he wanted to kill him when he walked in, but that didn't bother him. "Go see your mother," Jung-Soo ordered.

"I said I didn't want anyone to disturb us," Kang-Dae snapped.

"She hasn't seen either of you since before we left. Go. Explain the situation so she doesn't worry further. I'll stay with her." Kang-Dae looked back to Serenity. "Go," Jung-Soo noted how slowly he moved, almost weakly, as he reluctantly got out of the bed and walked out.

Alone with Serenity, Jung-Soo approached the bed. She didn't move at all. She wasn't sleeping, he could tell. He stood directly above her. "It's time to get up." No reaction. "You are Queen. You do not get to do this, not to yourself or to him." Still no reaction. "If you want to waste away so be it, but I will not allow you to take him with you." He could tell when she started listening. There was the smallest amount of eye movement beneath her closed lids.

"He has not eaten nor slept because he wants to care for you. As long as you are like this you will slowly kill you both." There was the slightest movement in her body at his words. "The longer you choose to suffer the longer he does as well. He's determined to share your pain." Jung-Soo paused, waiting for any type of response. A soft sniffle broke through the silence. Very soon after, a small sob left her which made him regret his harshness. "This is your home now," he spoke gently. "Whether you want it or not, you will live here for the remainder of your life. Is this how they would want you to live it?" He sat down next to her watching her closely.

"Do you know why I never returned to my home once Kang-Dae took me off the streets? I knew there was no home to return to. My village had been attacked shortly after I'd been sold off." He paused briefly. "I know what it is like to mourn a family. I know what it feels like to want to stop everything. I endured because I know who I am, and I know who they expected me to be. In that same way, I know who you are. I know you can and will endure this, and then you

169

will overcome it because you are a warrior Serenity. It is not in your heart to lay down and die. So live." Her shoulders shook as she quietly sobbed to herself. He gently touched her shoulder offering the only comfort he could. "This will not be your end, nor theirs. If they are anything like you, they too will endure." She wept openly now as he sat by letting her cry out all she had been holding back. He didn't interrupt her or try to calm her. He knew she had to release it all so she could begin to move on.

When Kang-Dae returned, Serenity was sitting up to his surprise. Jung-Soo said nothing to him as he passed him on his way out of the room. He was momentarily vexed, wondering what Jung-Soo could possibly have done, but quickly shifted his focus to her. He joined her on the bed, concern flooding him as he looked at her puffy red eyes. "What did he say to you?" he asked, ready to scold Jung-Soo for upsetting her at such a time. Serenity shook her head and sniffled. She was staring up at him, her eyes taking him in.

"You look so tired," she said hoarsely. Kang-Dae was about to dismiss her concerns, but she took his hand and tried to get him to lay down. He wouldn't at first, wanting to stay up with her. "Please?" Unable to deny her, he finally complied. She lay down as well, facing him so she could rest her hand on his cheek. He placed his atop of hers. "Sleep."

He didn't want to give into it. Now that she was actively interacting with him once more, he longed to stay up and speak with her, but the days hit him as soon as his head hit the pillow. Before he could allow himself to slip into unconsciousness, he spoke. "I was unable to keep my vow to you. But I swear, I will not allow you to face this alone. I will never leave you."

Sleep," she said once more. He was vaguely aware of her fingers stroking his hair as he finally succumbed to the darkness.

Serenity watched as Kang-Dae slept. When she actually looked at him, she realized the truth of his words. Kang-Dae had been suffering in solidarity with her. He looked like he had lost a bit of weight and his skin was a lot paler than normal. It hurt her heart to see him like this, especially since she knew she was the cause. She caressed his cheek. 'I'm sorry'. Jung-Soo was right, her mother would be disappointed to see her behaving this way. *'God doesn't let anything happen without purpose. It's how you endure it that determines whether you let it take you down or not.'* Her mother's words echoed in her mind, strengthening and saddening her. However, she chose to only embrace the strength. She would deal with her grief, but she wouldn't let it overwhelm her. If she was still here that meant she still had a purpose. She would pick herself up, not just for herself or Kang-Dae, but for her family as well. She toyed with her necklace. At some point during her depressive episode, Kang-Dae must have slipped it back on her. She held onto the jewel gaining strength from it. If this was to be her life from now on, she would not only live it, she would own it. After all, she was a queen.

CHAPTER TWENTY-FOUR

Kang-Dae awoke feeling better than he had in days. But when he saw he was alone in the bed, he popped up. He called out for Serenity, but quickly relaxed when he saw her at the table laying out food. She gave a small smile. Though it was tinted with sadness, it filled him with some relief as he was unsure when he would see her smile again.

"Morning or afternoon," she joked. "You were asleep for a long time." He moved to join her. "I asked Amoli to bring more chicken. I know you like that best," she said softly.

He wanted to ask her so many questions: how she was feeling, what she needed, but he feared he would only remind her of her pain So, he refrained. He, instead, settled for having a meal. He didn't touch his food for the longest time, too engrossed with watching her; glad to see her appetite had somewhat returned. Once she noticed he had yet to take a bite, she began to feed him a bite of hers. The whole scene felt like a dream to Kang-Dae. So much so, he began to question if he had ever awakened from his sleep. Serenity appeared to be starting to adjust to her loss, but he wanted to be cautious just in case she had a moment of relapse so he could be ready to be there for her. "You should meet with the council today."

"No. It is fine. Kyril can inform me later."

"You should go," she insisted. "You've been away too long. We both have. I'm going to meet with Nasim, and make sure the forts all have their provisions for the month," she said, surprising him once more.

"Are you sure?" She nodded.

"I want to get out of the room- do something useful." Kang-Dae watched her carefully, gauging her state for himself. She looked capable, but he had a twinge of doubt. He agreed to it anyway because it was what she wanted.

After finishing their meal, Serenity helped him dress, another pleasant surprise. She saw him off with a warm smile. Kang-Dae left the room praying this wasn't a fluke, but the beginning of what was to be their lives together.

When Min saw the King had emerged from his isolation, he was relieved. He'd been fearful the King would continue to neglect his duties in an effort to please the Queen. Now that it was clear she will be staying, he had to determine what the future looked like. And for the last couple of weeks, it had not looked good. His King was all out of sorts when it came to her. When he'd heard the King was taking the Queen on a trip, he knew exactly what he was planning. Min wanted to dissuade him from it, but he knew his King would not receive that well. He touched the scar on his nose. His injuries had healed some, but there was still some pain every now and then. The King's feelings for her overshadowed everything, including his senses. It made him fear for the King's and kingdom's future.

Amoli was helping her friend and fellow servant, Ah-Mei, bring in more silk into the workroom. Since the Queen had been in such a bad state for so long, Amoli had not been able to serve her as much as she used to. She wanted desperate to be around her Queen, but the King had insisted on her leaving them be. She had seen the way Serenity was as they returned from that's night. Her Queen had suffered a great loss. Amoli wanted to help her through it badly. However, until the King allowed it, she could do nothing but attend to her other duties. Ah-Mei followed behind Amoli. As they approached the materials rack, she'd had a misstep due to the pile of silk blocking her sight and she fell over. The silk in her hand went flying landing on the still drying fabric hanging to the right. Ah-Mei rushed to remove it before it became stained with the dye, but it was too late. Amoli quickly deposited her materials and went over to her. Ah-Mei looked almost white with fear. "I didn't mean to."

"I know. Here give it to me. We may be able to fix it if we wash it in time."

"Ah-Mei!" the loud and scratchy voice of the workshop's overseer caused both women to freeze. The older woman stomped over to them. She snatched the cloth from Amoli's hands and inspected it with a scowl. "Stupid girl! This silk was worth more than you. You are always causing trouble. I should have had you beaten from here long ago!" Amoli could do nothing but watch helplessly as the woman berated her friend. "You have no purpose here or anywhere. If you want to help your family, you would do more as a corpse than the way you are now."

Amoli watched as something went out in Ah-Mei's eyes. They became dull and lifeless. "Madam is right," she spoke in a calm yet cold tone. "Ah-Mei is unworthy of this life." The overseer was quiet, probably just as unsettled by her tone and words as Amoli was. Ah-Mei stepped forward and the overseer stepped back. Bewildered by her friend's behavior, she only watched as Ah-Mei made her way to the closest workstation and grabbed one of the knitting needles. Amoli screamed out as Ah-Mei raised her needle high and rushed over, desperate to stop her.

***

"Final count for boots was only 4500. We still need another 1600." Nasim nodded in agreement.

"The shoemakers fell behind due to a late shipment of supplies. The rest should be coming in by the next week." Nasim explained.

"That's good," Serenity said.

"My Queen, we may need to send more medical supplies to the fort in Hansi."

"Why, what happened?"

"Their food supply was contaminated. Many men fell ill, several died."

Serenity blinked, not believing she was completely unaware of this. "How did that happen?"

"We are unsure. It is still being investigated, but nothing has been found. It is possible that it was just an unfortunate occurrence."

"Random or not it should not have happened," declared Serenity, feeling traces of guilt. She should have been on top of this, but she'd been too busy feeling sorry for herself. "From now on, everything that goes out needs to be checked before it is shipped."

"Yes, my Queen."

"My Queen!" The sudden shout turned both Serenity and Nasim's attention to the young maid running up to them. Panting and red-faced, she fell to her knees before Serenity. "My Queen, come quickly, it's Amoli!" Fear gripped at her hearing Amoli's name. She didn't hesitate to follow the servant. Numerous scenarios went through her mind as

Serenity began to fear the worse. 'Please God, I can't handle anything else right now.'

The servant took her all the way to the back of the palace where the seamstresses worked. As she entered, she saw a line of female servants standing around whispering and staring at something. As soon as one of the women spotted Serenity, she announced her arrival causing all the women to turn and go to their knees. Ignoring all of them she headed past the crowd and stopped short. Her eyes widened at the scene before her.

Serenity couldn't comprehend the blood covering her friend at that moment. Frozen in shock she could barely think let alone speak. Amoli was seated by the corpse of a fairly young woman. The large knitting needle sticking out of her neck was making Serenity feel sick. Another woman dressed in grey and yellow- signifying her role as an overseer- stood by, looking as shocked as Serenity felt.

"I- I didn't mean-," the woman stammered. Serenity snapped out of her daze and carefully made her way over to Amoli, doing her best to avoid the large puddle of blood. She knelt down beside Amoli.

"Amoli," she called out to her gently. Amoli slowly looked at her, tears staining her cheeks. Amoli's face crumbled and she threw her arms around Serenity. Serenity held her as she wept.

When Kang-Dae arrived he too was stopped by the sight in front of him. When one of the servants reported that Serenity had gone to deal with a matter involving a dead servant, he'd rushed over as fast as he could. He'd been fearful it had been Amoli, but seeing her safe provided little relief when taking in the body of another young woman. He recognized her as one of the servants who would clean his study regularly. She had always seemed like a sweet girl. Kang-Dae ordered his men to have someone come and remove the body.

Kang-Dae turned his attention to the overseer and demanded an explanation. "I-I, don't know why she did this. She was a very troubled girl."

"Liar!" Amoli screamed out wrenching herself from Serenity's arms. She pushed herself up and pointed her finger in the woman's face. "You were always so mean to her: calling her names, telling her how useless. She was giving her ridiculous tasks and punishing her when she couldn't fulfill them." Amoli snatched the woman by the arm and forced her closer to the body. "You told her she was better off dead- now look at her! Look at her!" Serenity quickly pulled Amoli off the woman. She gave Kang-Dae a look. He nodded in understanding. Serenity led the hysterical Amoli away.

Kang-Dae turned his attention to the overseer who dropped to her knees.

"My King, I swear I did no harm to that girl. I may have been too harsh with her a few times, but it never bothered her this badly."

"Stop talking," commanded Kang-Dae effectively silencing the ranting woman. "Have her removed from the palace. She's never to set a foot inside these grounds again,"

"My King, please! I meant her no harm!" She screamed as the guards dragged her away. Looking at the remaining blood on the floor Kang-Dae shook his head sadly.

"Have someone clean up. We'll close down the workshop for a couple of days off. Tell everyone to go home." he ordered.

"Yes, my King."

***

"How is Amoli?" Kang-Dae asked.

"Devastated. I had to have Mehdi give her something to help her sleep. Please tell me that woman is gone."

"I've had her expelled from the grounds."

"Good." When Amoli had calmed a little, she told Serenity how the woman berated Ah-Mei regularly. But according to Amoli, she had never let it bother her before. Amoli described the girl as kind and happy most of the time. It was only these past few weeks did her personality begin to change. Amoli said she'd become short-tempered and sad. Amoli lamented the two had argued earlier in the week and they stopped speaking for a few days. The younger girl had apologized saying she hadn't been feeling well. Since then, Amoli had been helping her with her duties.

"I will have her body sent home along with a formal apology. She worked in our home and I failed to have her properly looked after. They should be compensated, though I fear nothing will ever replace what they lost."

"No, it won't," Serenity said solemnly. "but it's the least we can do." The sight of that poor girl's body wouldn't leave her brain. She was so young, but she'd been beaten down so much she didn't think she could get up again. The feeling was all too familiar to Serenity. Just a few days ago she could directly relate to it. The sick soldiers, a suicide, her inability to return home- Serenity didn't know if she could handle anymore misfortune.

CHAPTER TWENTY-FIVE

Serenity was helping with the preparations for the Gi family celebration. It was a nightmare and made her want to pull her hair out in frustration. She would much rather be with Amoli. She was still grieving the loss of her friend. Serenity had to force her to take the week off and visit her family for a bit. She missed her, but Serenity knew she needed some time away with those that loved her. She had been a bit envious of her in that regard, but she put that feeling aside and focused on other things; like this already fury inducing event. She would be lying if she said she only agreed to be involved in the first place because she wanted to and not because she had no plans to be here for any of it, thinking she would have been home by now. Jae-Hwa was getting on her last nerve and her father was one demand away from catching a beating. They kept wanting more and more extravagant things that Serenity would not agree to.

How those two could ignore the fact that they had been this close to a famine was beyond her.

"I have already told you what we are willing to offer you. If it bothers you so much, we can always cancel the whole thing." A flash of rage came across Jae-Hwa's face, but she was quick to cover it with a false smile. Yoon, on the other hand, was turning red.

"How could you even suggest such a thing?" He demanded, outraged, his bushy eyebrows almost meeting.

"Father calm down. I am sure the Queen did not mean to make such an impulsive statement." Jae-Hwa spoke calmly, but she was purposely projecting enough so that those around would be privy to their conversation. Serenity gave her a hard stare.

"I absolutely meant it."

"My Queen," she began, her condescending tone coming through. "A house name celebration has been a tradition in our land for years. I know, as a foreigner, there are some things about our ways that are strange to you, but there are some things the people expect and look forward to."

'The audacity of this woman,' Serenity thought. "Lady Gi," Serenity addressed her in the same manner Jae-Hwa had. "Our country is being invaded. Every day we come closer and closer to war. I think ensuring the safety and well-being of our people is more important to them than a party."

"Our people?" Yoon scoffed, causing Serenity to cut her eyes at him. Arezoo, Nasreen, and Gyrui- who had been hanging back- all took a step forward. But Serenity stopped them. The man's hatred of her was nothing new and she refused to waste any of her or anyone else's time dealing with it.

"The country is about to be at war. I think all our time, energy, and resources, could be used for better things.

For tradition's sake, I am willing to allow this event to go on, but it will be on my terms. If that is an issue, you are more than welcome to pay for everything. I am sure the King would not mind." Yoon stood with his mouth open like a fish, almost as if he were unable to process what she was telling him. Jae-Hwa's false smile had dimmed leaving only a blank expression. Though people around them appeared busy, it was obvious all of their attention was on the three of them. After several moments of tense silence, the hateful man stormed off with Jae-Hwa following behind him. Arezoo let out a string of insults that made Serenity laugh. "Couldn't agree more."

Kyril was suddenly next to her. "My Queen," he greeted.

"Hi, Kyril," she returned cheerfully.

"Have they put the crown in debt yet?" Serenity laughed.

"Not yet."

"What are their demands?"

"They wanted some troop to perform from Ghalia. They wanted to use royal funds to pay to bring them over." Kyril rolled his eyes.

"I told them they can pay for it themselves if they want it so bad."

"I am sure they eagerly volunteered," he said sarcastically.

"Oh, of course," she replied in the same tone. The two laughed.

"There's a local troop in the city. They'll come just for two silvers and a good meal. I will reach out to them."

"You don't have to," Serenity told him, not wanting him to inconvenience himself for them. Kyril shrugged it off.

"It'll take some of their ire off you. Besides, they're not that good, so that should make for an entertaining night."

Serenity let out a gasp of shock before chuckling. "Lord Kyril, when did you get so devious?"

"It is a hidden trait, I assure you."

"Thank you for helping me with this. I know there are a million more important things you could be doing."

"My duty is to serve you and my King. As long as I am useful, I will continue to do so." Serenity appreciated it and him. With half the council still against her, it was nice to have the member Kang-Dae trusted most in her corner.

"Have you had any trouble sending out rations?"

"Not as of yet. So far, we have only been able to go to the smaller villages. We don't have enough men to spare to go into the city. They have to come out to us and a lot of them are unable. I also wanted to send some out to those closer to the blockade. They're worse off than us, but Kang-Dae thinks it might be too much of a risk."

"It is a difficult situation. I may be able to help."

"Really?" she asked hopefully.

"I will speak to Amir; see if we can spare some men between the two of us. We will put it out to the council as well to see if anyone else would like to help."

"Thank you, Kyril. That would great."

Later that evening, when she informed Kang-Dae of what had happened between her, Yoon and Jae-Hwa, she had to stop him from going to confront the two right then. She honestly didn't care what the man said, or what he thought of her. After what she went through it all seemed laughable now. One party to appease a couple of narcissists was child's play. Besides, excluding the fact that it was in celebration of people she couldn't stand, it might be a fun evening. She could use a bit of fun.

"Kyril is helping her organize this charitable act of hers," sneered Satori. "She's been told over and over that it is an unnecessary risk, and yet she continues. If it goes wrong, how many men do we lose in the process? Does she not realize we have to prioritize the countries needs for all our survival?"

"What are you expecting from a person like her? An ignorant leader makes ignorant decisions, to the detriment of all," Yu said. The two sat alone in the council room, a game between them. Satori made a move on the board.

"The king seems apprehensive about it, at least. Perhaps she doesn't have him completely under her control."

"Don't be too sure. His actions have proven he will go to extremes for her. In any case, we should prepare ourselves if we need to intervene."

"Scheming again, are we?" Both men turned to see Kyril walking up to them. The men shared a look before turning back to him.

"Do you not have somewhere to be? Maybe preparing to scrub out the queen's chamber pot, since you're so willing to be at her service," mocked Satori turning his attention back to the game.

"Funny that a councilmember, who is sworn to serve, has such a low opinion of it. What exactly was your intention when you took the job?"

Satori fell silent, not liking the implication of his statement. He'd become a member to participate in making Xian a prosperous nation- like his father before him. It had been what he'd wanted from day one and he would continue to work for it as long as he served on the council. He may have been a young child during the war in the southern province, but he remembered the toll it had taken

195

on his grandfather and father. It had been a bitter campaign that had ended up taking his grandfather's life. All because of the whims of an incompetent ruler. When he was working to be a valued member of the court, he'd thought himself blessed to be under such a wise king. His fear of history repeating receded the more time he spent under his leadership. The King's death had been a devastating blow, but he thought that things would be alright under Kang-Dae. He was his father's son after all, and he would have Satori and other members for guidance. But he was stubborn, unwilling to really listen to what was best for Xian. He had the idealness of his father, but lacked the experience. Satori had always tried to take charge in hopes the young prince could learn from him and grow into a strong ruler, but he seemed to fight him at every turn. Now that he had married, he no longer listened to anyone. Satori feared for his country's future with every passing day.

"Don't question my loyalty. My family has served this country for generations. While yours… yours fought against the crown," Satori reminded Kyril.

Kyril gave a half-smirk. "Ah, yes, my father did love telling stories about defeating your family in battle. I'm sure your grandfather died honorably." Satori jumped up ready to charge at Kyril only to be stopped by Yu.

"Why are you here?" Yu demanded.

"I wanted to offer you a chance to be the loyal man you claim to be by helping the people."

"You mean helping the Queen," Satori spat.

"Why must you separate the two?" Kyril sighed. Satori narrowed his eyes. "We can come up with a successful plan together, if you are willing."

"If you want to risk your men, you're welcome to. I will not," Satori replied.

"Why don't you try caring about the people you always claim you're working for? If we leave the north to fend for themselves, Katsuo gains followers. Is it not better to show the people who will fight for them and keep them safe?" Satori didn't want to, but he considered Kyril's words. He was not wrong. And he had never wanted to abandon the people. But the risk had always been too high.

"What is your plan?"

CHAPTER TWENTY-SIX

Kang-Dae had just left his study, another headache grating on him. He was about to go lay down when Hui came running up to him with a distressed look on his face. 'What is it now?' he thought to himself. "My King, someone has ransacked the medicines!" Kang-Dae rubbed at his temple. He didn't want to deal with this now.

"What was taken?" he asked impatiently.

"It's hard to say. A lot of it was in the secured chest where I keep the more dangerous items," Hui explained.

"Someone stole poison from you?" Kang-Dae questioned.

"It would appear so, my King."

He shut his eyes in frustration. "Find out who was seen around the area today."

"I already know, my King,"

"And?"

"The Queen."

Kang-Dae went stock still. "What exactly are you trying to say?" He asked slowly.

"Nothing my King. I just thought you should know-"

"Know what?" Kang-Dae growled, losing patience. Hui began to stammer.

"I was just reporting what was told to me. I did not mean to accuse the Queen," he said. Kang-Dae's fists clenched at his sides, his anger pulsing within him at the mere suggestion of Serenity's culpability.

"I suggest you look into another suspect."

Hui nodded. "Yes, my King," He said quickly before scurrying away. Kang-Dae tried to dispel his anger, but he couldn't. The idea that Hui, or anyone, would try to implicate Serenity for something so nefarious was infuriating. He knew his focus should be on the thief and their plans for whatever was taken, but he was far too angry.

He went into the room hoping seeing Serenity would provide him with some peace. She was quietly reading on the daybed. The sight managed to quell some of his fury. Her emotional state had improved greatly lately. She smiled more, but still not as much as before. She was being affectionate with him little by little. They had not reached the same level of intimacy as they'd had before for that night, but Kang-Dae wasn't disappointed. To her, resuming their relationship was a final seal that she would live out her days here. Kang-Dae knew she wasn't ready to completely accept it just yet. It was alright, Kang-Dae had no problem waiting on her. Even if she never kissed him again, he would be fine. The most important thing was her happiness. What he wanted didn't matter.

Serenity noticed him watching her. She stared at him only for a second before asking, "Is it your head again?" He was impressed at her ability to read him so well in such a short time. He nodded. She put her book down and beckoned him over. He laid his head in her lap as she gently took it in her hands and rubbed at his temples. It was a small relief, but the action itself was what meant so much to him. She was taking care of him. Though he didn't deserve it, he could never reject it. "Saranghae," he said to her.

"You still haven't told me what that means," she said. He took one of her hands and laid a soft kiss on her fingers.

"Keep studying," was all he said.

***

"It isn't working. He's become even more loyal to her. He won't even consider investigating her involvement in the theft," Yoon spoke to his co-conspirator.

"The expectation was not that he would suspect her right away. The main goal was to plant the notion. Once everything begins to come out, he'll begin questioning everything about her," the man answered.

"With their excursion to Kah Mah coming up, the King will not be within our reach. It'll set us back."

"Once they return, we'll increase his exposure. In the meantime, their absence will grant us an opportunity to mold the people's opinion of their Queen. We can start in the palace, poison the nobles against her. They will be the easiest to turn."

CHAPTER TWENTY-SEVEN

Serenity's feet refused to move. In her absentmindedness, she'd forgotten that going on this adventure required getting on a ship. More importantly: facing the water. She'd honestly thought she would be okay since she had braved the lake that night when she thought she was going home. But she supposed it was her desperate desire to see her family that had helped her overcome it. Without that, the fear had returned full force and now it was accompanied by that soul-crushing sorrow as the memories of that night resurfaced. If she could just make it to the ship, she would be fine. But one step onto the dock had left her paralyzed. She could almost feel that coldness seeping in once more. That horrible feeling of her body being completely at the mercy of the rough river had emerged causing her heart to race erratically.

'I can't do this,' she thought, taking a step back right into Kang-Dae's chest. "Shut your eyes." She felt the rumble of his voice as he spoke. Suddenly turning back to look at him seeing his warm brown eyes staring down at her. "Do it," he prompted. She obeyed without question. As soon as she did, she felt herself being lifted. Her arms instantly reached out to wrap around his neck. Even though she could no longer see the water below, knowing she was heading over it continued to fill her with dread. She clung to him a bit tighter. "Did you know you talk in your sleep?" Serenity moved her head to where she assumed Kang-Dae's face was.

"What?"

"You talk in your sleep. Very interesting things, I must say."

Confused as to why he was bringing up this obvious lie, she retorted, "no I don't."

"Yes, you do. I do not know what you were dreaming about last night, but I believe you said something about catching the flying poodle because it was too cute to live."

Serenity's jaw dropped. She didn't recall having any dreams last night, let alone one where she had homicidal tendencies toward small dogs.

"I -I didn't," she continued to protest weakly.

"What exactly is a poodle and how does it fly? Do you normally try to kill things that are deemed too cute in your world?" He asked only making her embarrassment that much stronger.

"No! And I didn't say that that!" she whined, burying her face in his neck to hide her embarrassment.

"I am very certain you did."

"Did not."

"You did."

"No, I didn't"

"But you did."

She opened her eyes so she could look him in the eyes before killing him, only to pause when she saw they were no longer outside. Inside what she assumed was their cabin on the ship, she stared up at him with confused eyes while he just smiled.

"We are here." he set her down gently, although she still had to study herself due to the movements of the ship. She was shocked that he'd managed to carry her the entire way and kept her from him thinking about her overwhelming fears. She wrapped her arms around him.

"Thank you," she said so grateful for his actions- grateful for him. He responded with a kiss on top of her head.

The trip to Kah Mah was not a long one, which was good because Serenity didn't know how long she could stay cooped up below deck. She was unwilling to take a chance of going above. She entertained herself with books she'd brought, braiding her hair (she even taught Kang-Dae, so he could help her), stories from Kang-Dae's childhood, and long dinner conversations with Amir who'd joined them on their trip. Amir's father was from Kah Mah, so he knew the language and culture better than Kang-Dae. He had insisted on accompanying them, wanting to help with the negotiations. Serenity enjoyed his company, having not spent too much time with the youngest councilmember. He was more mild manner than the rest and seemed to lack a bit of confidence here and there, but he was kind and clever. According to Kang-Dae, his father had grown ill and wanted Amir to take his position. Kang-Dae allowed it because he had grown up with Amir and knew he would do the job well.

After only two days of sailing, they docked. The first thing Serenity saw when she opened her eyes while still in Kang-Dae's arms was a line of people before them. They were dressed for the warm weather. Though the soldiers wore armor, their arms and legs were still exposed. The few women with them didn't wear the many layers that she had been subjected to all these months. The off-shoulder wraps were fitted above a wrap skirt that was brought together with a large sash. Kang-Dae put Serenity behind him protectively while his guard stood in front of both of them. The soldiers in front of them had their hands resting on the hilts of their swords and more than a few of them had bows out with the arrows in a resting position. The man who stood in front of them yelled something in an unfamiliar language. Serenity looked up at Kang-Dae for help, but she could see he was just as confused as she was. The leader repeated himself more aggressively. The guards tensed and their hands went to their weapons. The soldiers unsheathed their swords and several prepared to release their arrows.

Amir's voice rang out, speaking what seemed to be the same language back to them. The leader paused. Serenity clung to Kang-Dae's arm. 'God, please don't let me have brought us here just to die.' The standoff lasted only a few seconds, but it felt much longer. The leader gave his men a sign with his hand and they all put their weapons down. Amir spoke again, gesturing to Kang-Dae and her. The leader moved toward them. The man looked at the guard expectantly. Kang-Dae, figuring out what the man wanted, gave the order for his men to stand down. Once all weapons were away, the line of soldiers parted and a woman, looking to be in her late thirties with tanned skin, came through. She had a gold headpiece atop her head. Her style of dress matched the women around her, but the colors she wore were brighter. The line of men bowed as she came by. Amir stepped forward before he started speaking once more. The woman held up her hand to stop him.

"Welcome to Ka-Mah. I am Prija, daughter of the late King Shin," she said in very good English. Kang-Dae took Serenity's hand in his.

"Thank you for meeting us." The queen nodded.

"We have prepared a place for you and your people where you can rest well from your journey. Tonight, we will have a great feast to celebrate your arrival," Queen Prija informed them. "I hope you find our home most welcoming." With that said, she turned and began walking off, her men trailing behind her. A couple of the women hung back to lead Kang-Dae and Serenity. Exchanging looks, the couple followed behind.

The place that was prepared for them was a private wing in the palace. It was relatively smaller than their own, but no less extravagant. The main hall was housed in a very large building with multiple dark brown rooves stacked on top of one another. The wooden walls were colored yellow. There were two smaller structures on both sides, but with similar designs. Gold statues sat at the entrances.

Their room was moderately sized, and the bed had a large tapestry above it with sheer green curtains falling around it. Serenity was delighted to see she had been given several dresses and outfits for her stay. 'Goodbye, hundred-layer dresses,' she thought to herself gleefully. Kang-Dae hadn't been too thrilled, especially with the ones that exposed a small part of her stomach, feeling it was a bit inappropriate. But Serenity just argued that she couldn't turn her nose up at gifts from the people they were asking for help from. After she had tried one on, his tune had changed considerably. The red and gold dress she wore was fitted, showing off the curves of her body. Completely sleeveless and strapless her arms were bare, allowing the breeze to cool her just right. The dress had a sewn on sash that lay on her left shoulder and fell behind her, reaching her thigh. Circles of gold were belted around her waist.

The look Kang-Dae was giving her when she emerged brought butterflies to her stomach. She felt naked under his dark stare. Clearing her throat, she reminded him about dinner. He approached her slowly, his eyes never losing their lustful glint. Serenity swallowed hard as his arm slid around her waist, making her shiver. "At dinner, I will be sure to thank the queen for her generosity," he said huskily.

Serenity was blushing like crazy. "We're going to be late," she told him trying to redirect his attention from her. Kang-Dae smirked and leaned down to kiss her. Serenity turned at the last second, missing the disappointed look on his face. "Come on. We need to go," she claimed pulling him by the arm and heading for the door.

The hall they were brought to had high ceilings with a beautiful gold chandelier in the shape of a rose hanging from the ceiling. There were no chairs, only mats for everyone to sit on at the low tables. Queen Prija arrived last, after the food had been set out. Everyone stood as she answered. Serenity wasn't sure what the protocol was when two monarchs meet one another, so she followed Kang-Dae's lead. When he stood, she stood. He, however, did not bow the way that others had; so, she followed suit. Once

Queen Prija sat, everyone else did as well and it wasn't until she took her first bite that everyone began eating. Serenity looked at the different food around her, not sure where to start. Kang-Dae sensed her apprehension and offered her something he thought she'd like. Trusting him, she accepted it and wasn't disappointed.

"I was surprised when our look-out spotted your ships. I wasn't sure you would come. When I first received word from your people, I thought it was a mistake." Queen Prija's low but commanding voice spoke causing the rooms to go silent.

"No mistake. It's been far too long since our two countries had any interactions," Kang-Dae said.

"This is true, our nations were great allies long ago."

"I see no reason why it cannot be so once more," suggested Kang-Dae, laying the ground for them to make their plea.

Queen Prija let out a soft chuckle. "I believe our predecessors would disagree."

"They are not us," Kang-Dae replied. Serenity's eyes shifted back and forth between the two monarchs. Queen Prija took a sip from her cup. Everyone slowly began to focus on the food before breaking into their own conversations. Serenity placed her hand on Kang-Dae's knee.

"Let's give it some more time," she whispered in Xianian. Kang-Dae wanted to continue to press, but decided to take Serenity's suggestion. They continued their meal and awaited their opportunity.

After dinner, they were ushered into another hall. This one housed a gorgeous and enormous chair that sat atop multiple steps. A long beige carpet made a path from the chair to the doors. Kang-Dae and Serenity were asked to the front. Queen Prija stared down at them from her throne. Not wanting to draw things out any longer, Kang-Dae began.

"We would like to begin anew in our international relations."

"Oh, and why is that?" Queen Prija inquired.

"Do we need to say?" challenged Kang-Dae.

The Queen smiled. "No, I suppose you do not. Even in our isolation, we make a point to know what is going on out there so we can prepare if dangers are close to our shores."

"They will not touch your lands," Kang-Dae said.

"I'm sure you believe that, but we have not prospered this long without being cautious."

"That is reasonable."

"What about what you ventured here for? Is that reasonable?" she questioned.

"We could use your assistance. It will become difficult to keep our people fed during this time. We would like to come to an agreement that can benefit both our people," offered Kang-Dae.

"And what would that be?"

"Let's us open our borders back up for trade on both sides. For so many years we've broken off our mutual trading. It's left us both lacking in one aspect or another. I know it is hard for you all to maintain your homes and structures with your limited amount of lumber and stone. I also know steel is in short supply here. We can begin to once more provide each other with things we need and grow stronger together as we had before."

Queen Prija's expression did not change. She played with the armrest of her throne while staring at them. "This is not a small request," she said.

"No, it is not, but it can change things for the better for each of us," stated Kang-Dae.

"You speak of renewing our relationship. Did you know back in those days, a request such as this demanded a show of strength to demonstrate the resolve of the one making the requests?"

"I recall my father telling of the tradition," Kang-Dae responded cautiously.

"The requester had a choice between performing a series of tasks or facing an opponent of the sitting king or queen's choice. If they failed at either task, their request would be denied, and they would be required to offer tribute. I think this would be a good way to re-open negotiations between us."

'Is she serious?' Serenity thought.

"You do?" Kang-Dae asked.

"Yes, an act of goodwill between nations. The people would love to see it. If you are as genuine in your offer as you appear, I am sure you will succeed."

'Was this woman trying to set them up?' The entire offer sounded disingenuous to Serenity. Maybe she was still holding a grudge for her family's sake. Serenity didn't want Kang-Dae to agree, but she knew he would. He was not someone who backed down, especially if it was for his country.

"If that is what you wish, I will agree," Kang-Dae declared.

"Wonderful. We will have the match two days from now," Queen Prija announced. She stood and every attendant took a knee. "I hope you will not feel confined to these walls during your stay. Our home is a lovely and lively place. You should go out and enjoy it." Her tone stayed the same, never shifting or changing inflection. Kang-Dae bowed his head and Serenity did the same. The queen walked down the steps. Kang-Dae swung Serenity over to his side as she passed. The woman never broke her stride or looked their way as she made her way to the door. Everyone followed behind her in a single file line spanning the length of the room, which almost made Serenity laugh. The last to leave, Kang-Dae took Serenity's hand in his as he led them out. From his grip, she could tell he was tense. This was not the way they expected things to go.

***

Jung-Soo looked over each man before him. All of them were sporting an injury or wound "How many were there?" he questioned.

"At least fifty, sir. They came out of nowhere. We didn't hear them until they were right on us. They must have been waiting for us."

It was a story he'd heard before. That made two transports of food stolen by bandits in the past week. Soldiers reported traveling on the road to drop off provisions for civilians, only to be attacked before they could reach their destination. Both times men's lives were lost, and the food was taken. The way the survivors described their fighting style and weapons, Jung-Soo doubted they were ordinary bandits. That was not the most disturbing thing. As more and more houses began to involve themselves in charity, there were many carts of food leaving the palace regularly, off to different parts of the nation to help those in need. Both parties that had been targeted so far were organized by Serenity herself. With it only being two attacks, Jung-Soo wanted to wait before he drew any conclusions. But he didn't like how it was looking. It seemed she was specifically being targeted, but to what end? With both her and Kang-Dae off in Kah-Mah, Serenity had placed him in charge of her project. He needed to figure this out and

soon.

CHAPTER TWENTY-EIGHT

The weapon in his hands was not one he was familiar with. The curved blade at the end of the staff was of a unique design. They dressed him in their outfits which were lighter than what he was used to. He felt a bit more exposed, but at least his speed wouldn't be affected. His feet were bare, allowing him to feel the sand on the ground. The arena was a not so large circle. There was a large chair raised up for the Queen and a few benches for Serenity, Amir and other important guests, while everyone else was forced to sit on the grass. Kang-Dae's gaze drifted to Serenity, who was sitting next to the Queen. He could see her performing her habit of nervously playing with their hands even from a distance, causing him to smile to himself. He wasn't foolish enough to believe this would be an easy victory. Queen Prija's goal was for him to lose. His opponent would be skilled. He would have to be more defensive than offensive at first to gauge his fighting style. It will give him a better advantage. Xian needed him to win, so he would. The small crowd began to shout as the military leader, Su, entered the circle. Su had been the one who met them at the dock. Kang-Dae wasn't surprised. Queen Prija clearly trusted him with her military forces. She wouldn't have put him up to the task if she didn't have confidence in him. This was a delicate situation. He needed to win, but given Queen Prija and the people's low opinion of Xian already, he couldn't make things worse either. Su grabbed his weapon, a bladed staff, and took his stance directly in front of Kang-Dae. The people grew silent. Kang-Dae tightened his grip on his weapon. A shout echoed through the air and Su was suddenly coming at him. 'I guess we've begun.'

Serenity tensed as Su charged at Kang-Dae with a yell. Kang-Dae was fast, dodging him while keeping him in his sights. The man was not deterred and quickly spun around aiming his staff right at Kang-Dae's head. Kang-Dae used his weapon to take the brunt of the hit. Su immediately swung again at his torso, but Kang-Dae managed to jump back just in time. Su was relentless- attacking nonstop, but Kang-Dae managed to block every hit. Serenity was beginning to feel sick. This was not like those sparring sessions between him and Jung-Soo. Though neither man appeared to hold back against one another, they were never this brutal. Serenity noticed Kang-Dae wasn't attacking nearly as much as he usually did. In fact, he had not attempted one hit yet. 'Maybe he has a plan,' she thought. She glanced at Queen Prija whose expression gave nothing away. She appeared neither nervous nor confident. Serenity thought she should probably be doing the same, but she was way too anxious to fake it.

Su swung at his head once more and Kang-Dae dodged it. Su looked to be getting frustrated. And from the way he was panting, he was getting tired as well. Before Kang-Dae could use it to his advantage, he noticed a change in Su's demeanor. Something in his eyes changed and his body relaxed. He looked as if he were going to take a step back, but Kang-Dae didn't let his guard down. When Su came forward once more with his arms raised, Kang-Dae immediately raised his staff to block only for Su to slide his staff behind Kang-Dae's. He pulled with such force that Kang-Dae's strong hold on his staff was used against him and Su was able to toss him over his shoulder onto the ground. Momentarily stunned, Kang-Dae was unable to block the swift hit to his head with the blunt end of Su's staff. The pain was immediate and intense, but the dizziness and disorientation were worse. He struggled to get his bearings; but before he could, he saw the staff coming for him again. He was able to roll out of the way. As he struggled to get up, a kick to his stomach sent him back to the ground. Kang-Dae coughed out his pain as he struggled to breathe. Showing no mercy, Su slammed staff into Kang-Dae's stomach that had yet to recover from his previous blow. Aching and coughing,

Kang-Dae turned to his side trying to relieve his pain and avoid another hit. He felt Su kicking his back and Kang-Dae grunted. With a move too fast for Kang-Dae to notice, Su sliced at Kang-Dae's chest cutting into his flesh. Kang-Dae held in his cry of pain and tried to get up, but was soon kicked over onto his back once more. Su stood above him and began to press his blade into his fresh wound. With a hiss Kang-Dae gripped the base of the staff, trying to keep the blade from sinking further. "Yield," Su demanded. "Protect what little honor you have."

'No honor, disgraceful, liar,' words that had been tormenting him for weeks reemerged with a vengeance, only now he could not shut them out. 'Dishonorable! Vow breaker! Liar!' The roar sounded through the air was almost inhuman. He didn't even realize it came from him.

It was only Amir's strong hand on Serenity's shoulders that kept her from jumping to her feet and demanding the fight be stopped. Watching Kang-Dae being thrown caused her anxiety to spike. Watching him so ruthlessly kicked while he was down had her wanting to run out into the arena herself, to hell with their rules. Amir, fortunately, had predicted her reaction and intervened quickly. She wanted to call out to Kang-Dae- tell him to surrender, but she stopped herself. She knew enough about Xianian culture to know that he would feel ashamed by such an act, so she bit her tongue. A sound rang out from the center of the circle that scared her. It was primal, frightful, and the fact that it came from Kang-Dae made it all the more disturbing. Su looked to be just as disturbed because he faltered just enough for it to be noticeable. Kang-Dae's hands tightened around the base of the spear. Using all his strength he pushed it upward causing the staff to hit Su right in the chin. He stumbled back with the yelp. Kang-Dae moved so fast, it shocked Serenity when he was suddenly in front of Su striking him right in the throat. Su staggered back clutching at his throat gagging and gasping out. Serenity wanted to feel relief that Kang-Dae now had the upper hand, but the look on his face gave her pause. He looked different: cold, merciless. As Su tried to recover, Kang-Dae snatched the staff from his hands and swept his legs out from underneath him. Su fell backward reaching out helplessly for something to hold onto only to grasp the air. The same way Su had stood ruthlessly above Kang-Dae, now Kang-Dae did the same. He tossed the staff to the side and stared down at Su with such contempt. Serenity had no idea where it came from. Kneeling, Kang-Dae delivered a blow to Su's nose that was so strong and brutal, Serenity could've sworn she heard the bone crack even from the distance. After the second hit, she didn't need to guess whether it was broken. The wet sound of his fists hitting the already demolished appendage would haunt her. But even worse than the sounds, was the look on Kang-Dae's face. The weird mixture of hatred and detachment as he continued to pulverize Su's face was hard to look at.

Queen Prija shouted a word in her language that echoed throughout the arena. Kang-Dae stopped mid-strike, his fist bloody. He slowly stood and backed away. The anger was still there, but he appeared to be containing it.

"This kind of brutality is not tolerated in Kah Mah." Serenity glared at her.

"You were the one who insisted on this fight. I didn't see you talking about brutality when it was my husband on the ground." Although Serenity had been appalled by Kang-Dae's behavior, she would not let this woman portray him as a ruthless brute when this whole thing was her idea. The Queen returned Serenity's harsh stare before giving an order to her men. Guards came out and helped Su up. Serenity hated the way everyone was looking at Kang-Dae... like he was a monster. This would not help their cause at all.

***

Jae-Hwa twirled gracefully about the floor, her long sleeves flowing in the breeze. The dancers circled her, in their light blue dresses, before separating into two lines. She walked the path between them while covering her face with her decorated fan. Keeping her face covered, she moved to the left allowing her arm to move to the music. She spun around, successfully switching the fan to her other hand, and repeated the same move to the right. She slowly lowered it to reveal her eyes while bending forward slightly. Applause sounded around her as the ladies watching expressed their approval. Jae-Hwa smiled graciously as she bowed.

"Beautiful, Lady Gi. You will dazzle everyone at the celebration," Lady Song praised.

"Thank you. I've been practicing for months." And she had. Although originally, she'd been hoping to catch the attention of the King. She wasn't sure that would be possible with that woman always at his side. "It should be a wonderful evening."

"I heard the queen has been helping you plan." Jae-Hwa purposely shifted her eyes.

"Yes, she has. She's been very kind to offer her assistance, even though she doesn't know much about planning an event such as this."

"She hasn't caused any issues has she?" One of the women asked.

"Oh no, no- of course not. The Queen is very willing. It's just," Jae-Hwa paused allowing her smile to dim somewhat. "As someone with her background, she's not very familiar with our traditions. Sometimes I feel she doesn't understand the importance of them. It's not her fault of course. Her culture is so different from ours. How could she understand?"

"As a queen, she should make time to. After all, if she has the title, she has to embody it. And that includes adhering to the people," Lady Song spoke up looking indignant on Jae-Hwa's behalf.

"I'm sure it's difficult for her, being so far from home," Jae-Hwa said in a weak attempt to defend her.

"Where is her home? I don't think I've ever heard where she's from," Lady Pei asked.

"I haven't either. Strange, isn't it?" questioned Lady Song.

"Very. There are so many questionable lands out there. Who knows what kind of place she hails from?"

"Do not be so suspicious. I'm sure the king wouldn't have taken her as a queen if he didn't trust her," Jae-Hwa insisted.

"I'm not so sure. Those foreign women are good at seducing men and getting them to do whatever they want while secretly using them," Lady Pei spoke. "You know, Lord Ji married a woman from Banal and she convinced him to send his entire fortune to her family back in her country. After that, she went to visit them and never came back. He was devasted." Jae-Hwa laughed off all their conjecture, but inside she was patting herself on the back.

CHAPTER TWENTY-NINE

Kang-Dae hissed as the cloth came into contact with his wound. Serenity winced in sympathy and gently blew on it hoping to relieve the sting. She wrapped it up as best she could. He wanted to have Mehdi do it, but with Kang-Dae still fuming from the fight, she thought it best not to subject the kindhearted medic to that. Kang-Dae cursed in Xianian. "She wanted this. She wanted to make us look like the enemy."

"She's not the one who had a fit of "roid rage" and almost beat a man to death." Kang-Dae raised his brow, not understanding the reference; but she didn't bother explaining. "You knew this was going to be a hard sell. The last thing we need is for them to have another reason to distrust us."

"Was I meant to just take it?"

"No, but you didn't need to go that far. You've been less brutal to men who were trying to kill you. I don't understand what made you so angry."

Kang-Dae looked away. He knew he had overreacted and risked destroying their possible alliance with Queen Prija. At that moment, however, he could think of nothing but silencing that voice- and Su had become his chosen target. The rage he felt had been blinding. He'd never experienced anything like it before. It had disturbed him as much as it had Serenity.

"We need to return. We cannot waste any more time here while Katsuo roams our lands."

"Yeah, that's kind of the reason why we came, to get help with that?" Serenity reminded him.

"Why are you only angry with me?" he asked, not liking how she was only blaming him.

"I'm not," she asserted. "I hated seeing you get hurt, but it's not about us."

He was silent for a few seconds before he finally released a sigh. She was right, and he knew it. He took her hand in his. "I am sorry. I let my pride get in the way of our goal. It was foolish." Serenity squeezed his hand.

"You know, I'm not the only one you need to apologize to." Kang-Dae groaned.

"I should have just killed him." Serenity slapped him on the shoulder.

"I think you are much more violent than I am." The second hit was on his head.

"Ow!"

***

The next day, both husband and wife entered the main hall with their heads high. Despite their current situation, they refused to look weak. Making their way up to the throne, they stopped at the steps. As one, they bowed respectfully.

Kang-Dae spoke first, "I wish to offer my regrets and apologies for my behavior. It was inexcusable as a guest, and a king." He turned to Su, who was glaring at him from behind his wrapped, battered face. "I apologize to you for my actions that day. For the grievances I've caused, I offer myself as penance for my deeds. Whatever you want of me, you shall have it."

Just as Su looked as though he were about to spit out words Serenity knew would not be of forgiveness, Queen Prija interrupted. "That will not be necessary. As your Queen pointed out, it was a match that I set in motion. I must take some responsibility as well." Uncertainty crossed both Serenity and Kang-Dae's faces. "Our customs are not yours, neither are our expectations or morals." From the corner of her eye, Serenity could see Kang-Dae's jaw clench at her passive-aggressive dig. "We should not expect those from other lands to adhere to the same conduct and principles as us. After all, there were reasons why we parted ways in the past." Serenity did not like where this was going, and neither did Kang-Dae because he began to speak.

"Queen Prija, I would hope you would not hold my people accountable because of my actions and those who came before me. I believe what is coming is much greater than all of these things."

"What is coming has nothing to do with Kah Mah. And it would be a failure of my leadership to allow Xian to put that trouble on us." Kang-Dae's anger was so strong Serenity could almost feel it. She squeezed his hand in an attempt to keep him calm. Turning to her, she could see the frustration. Without speaking she silently reminded him of the importance of staying calm.

"You may not be the same arrogant king who thought to impose his will on all those around him, but it is clear to me you are of the same stock."

'Hell no.' Serenity was not going to let this woman try to shame Kang-Dae. She wanted to let loose on her. But just as she had done before, Kang-Dae reminded her not to give in to her anger with a light squeeze. He shifted his eyes to the Queen, and then back to her, giving a subtle shake of his head.

Kang-Dae released her hand and dropped to his knees, shocking everyone in the room- and leaving Serenity flabbergasted. She had never seen him take such a position before. Judging from the reactions of everyone in the room, it was just as unheard in Kah Mah as well. She fought against the need to pull him back up, hating to see him humbling himself in such a way.

"On behalf of myself and those before me, I plead with you, Queen Prija, for forgiveness. I would never ask or try to force you to return as a nation of Xian, for I know you are a strong and moral people who have earned your independence. On the contrary, it is us that needs you now. Though we have no right to ask, I do so in hopes we may start again as allies and equals." For the first time since their arrival, Queen Prija looked as though she had no idea what to do next. She was completely caught off guard. But beneath her shock, there was also disappointment-frustration.

'She wanted to make us look like the enemy,' Kang-Dae had said the other night. Serenity realized now that he'd been right. Kang-Dae's actions today jeopardized her plan. She hadn't invited them there to entertain any deal they had. She'd brought them to show her people an enemy; an enemy they could stand against without remorse.

"Queen Prija, may we talk alone?" Serenity blurted out. Kang-Dae didn't lift his head, but turned his eye toward her. "It's okay," she whispered, so only he could hear. Queen Prija hesitated for a moment before dismissing everyone, including Kang-Dae. Kang-Dae hadn't liked that and tried to linger holding on to her hand, but she reassured him with a smile. Patting his hand, she nudged him on. Reluctantly, he exited leaving the Queens alone.

CHAPTER THIRTY

Tense silence was all that was between the women, as the seconds went by. Serenity didn't have a plan for what she was about to say, but she felt she needed to speak with the woman; Queen to Queen.

"This isn't about your people's pride or some feud from years ago," Serenity said. Queen Prija crossed her legs and leaned back against her throne. "The deal was more than fair, and it would help your people. You do not seem the type to turn away from something that would benefit your country. Especially not over some disagreement you weren't even there for. The only way this hurts you, is if you already chose who to support in this war. The reason you know about Katsuo's attack is because he's already come to you. Am I right?" Queen Prija didn't look away, but held Serenity's gaze without shame.

"I do what is best for my country as always." Serenity wanted to grab the woman by her hair. "You are right. The grievances of the past matter very little to me, but the fate of our future is everything. I'm afraid that that future cannot involve Xian."

Serenity took a moment to collect herself and think of her next move, not wanting to speak in anger. "Do you know why we came?" The question seemed to throw the composed queen. "I mean do you know why we chose to come to you and not anyone else? Yes, you had the resources. But you aren't the only place we could go to for that." The Queen remained quiet. "They call me a seer, and not because of any superstitious beliefs. I do see the future."

"Then you should have known this endeavor would not succeed," Queen Prija said simply.

Not bothering to respond to that she continued. "My vision led me specifically here. I didn't understand at first, but now I think I get it. I think I understand what I saw."

"What was that?" she inquired, not seeming the least bit interested.

Serenity could tell she didn't believe her. Whether she thought she was lying or crazy was not clear, but it wasn't the first time Serenity had been in this position. She decided to let her vision speak for her. As she explained her dream, Queen Prija never changed her expression, but she continued to listen. When Serenity got to the part about the large figure in the distance and waking up speaking the word 'echang', her demeanor changed. Serenity saw her stiffen and she no longer looked so indifferent.

"I thought it meant we could help each other, but now I think it was a warning for you. Our country's fates are tied. If we fall, you will too. None of what you've done will protect you." Serenity didn't know where this was coming from. Her heart was pounding, and she fought to keep her voice from trembling. She still hadn't figured out the full meaning of that dream, but she was desperate. The Queen's gaze shifted slightly before looking back to Serenity.

"I appreciate your concern for both our countries, but my concern is only for mine. I cannot be frightened into risking my people's lives based on the word of a stranger."

Serenity didn't bother hiding her frustration. "Fair enough," she sighed. She turned to leave when she remembered something else in her dream. "He asked you for something didn't he- something you refused to give him? Something precious to your people?" This time she could not hide her shock. The way she clutched at her throne was a dead giveaway that Serenity's assumption had been correct.

"Next time, he won't ask." Serenity told her before bowing and moving toward the door.

"Queen Serenity," she called out to her. Serenity paused at the door.

"Your husband may not be as understanding about this. I hope he will not cause any issues while you are here."

"My husband will not know about any of this until we've left," Serenity assured her. "You all are about to go through a lot, I don't think I need to add to it." Not having anything else to say she left the room, leaving the queen to ponder over her choices.

Later that night, she felt like she'd failed as queen and seer. She lay with her head on Kang-Dae's chest, careful to avoid his injury from his match. "I'm sorry I brought us here for nothing," she lamented. Kang-Dae kissed the top of her head.

"It is not your fault. If she is too stubborn to help, we'll go somewhere else," he reassured.

"Satori's going to have a big laugh about this," Serenity mused bitterly. Kang-Dae gave her a comforting squeeze.

"Not if I have his mouth sewn up," he offered jokingly.

"Would you?"

"I will even let you hold the needle."

"You know I'm bad at sewing," she reminded him.

"All the better." Serenity snorted before burying her face in his chest as she laughed.

"Can we go home now?" She asked once she recovered. Briefly frozen after hearing Serenity use the term home to describe the palace for the first time, he felt his chest tighten. Serenity appeared to realize what she said because she too stopped moving. Kang-Dae feared she had upset herself and would begin to head back to a depression.

"We'll leave tomorrow." He said, hoping to distract her. She slowly nodded before snuggling back into him. He gently stroked the soft curls until she fell asleep. Kang-Dae listened to her steady breathing, finding comfort in her peace- a peace he hadn't had for a while. He'd not slept through the night in weeks. He was always on edge, fearing any moment she would fall back into despair. He was trying his best to keep her content, but he felt it would never be enough. He could never fill the hole in her heart left by the loss of her family. The weight of it was like a shadow that constantly hounded him, ever-present. He only ate when he was with her, and then it had become a chore as the taste of food was no longer appealing. Other than trying to make up for Serenity's loss, he found no pleasure in anything he'd used to; too distracted with intrusive thoughts. The moments he did sleep, they were filled with nightmares that only reminded him of what plagued him during the day. He kept this all to himself, never wanting Serenity to see the toll being taken on him. It was his burden to bear; it was his responsibility; it was his penance for failing to fulfill his vow.

CHAPTER THIRTY-ONE

The men were prepping the ship while Serenity waited by the shore, her back facing the ocean. Staring at the place in the distance, she couldn't help feeling disappointed with the way things had turned out. "The people of Kah Mah can be just as stubborn as Xianians," Amir said. "You must not blame yourself for how things turned out." Serenity gave a sad smile.

"I know, I just wish we could have helped each other."

"You did all you could. This will not be our end. I do not believe this trip was without purpose. A seed was planted, it just might take some time to sprout." Comforted by his wise words, Serenity felt a little better.

Kang-Dae made his way up to her, telling them that the ship was ready. Amir went ahead to board. Kang-Dae grinned before reaching for her, preparing to carry her on board when the sound of a loud shout caught their attention.

Military leader Su emerged from the tree line a group of soldiers following behind him. Serenity's fear gripped her as the men came forward. Had Prija decided to take this chance to remove Kang-Dae and gain Katsuo's favor? She cursed herself for not reporting what she knew to Kang-Dae the night before. Amir came rushing back, hoping to de-escalate whatever this was. Su walked up to them. Both Kang-Dae and Amir stood in front of her blocking her from his view. Scowling at Kang-Dae, Su turned to Amir and spoke. Amir's expressions shifted from caution to surprise and finally relief. Su handed something to him, speaking once more. He looked past both men to Serenity and gave a subtle nod to her before cutting his eyes at Kang-Dae and returning to his men.

"What did he say?" Serenity asked. Amir released a light chuckle and smiled.

"The queen wants to give us something as a sign of good faith."

Su's voice rang out and the men parted, revealing a trail of carts and wagons. "Queen Prija says this will be Kah Mah's first shipment. From now on, their docks will be open to us for trade." Serenity and Kang-Dae shared matching astonished expressions.

Amir handed Serenity the book he'd received from Su. "She also wanted you to have this." Serenity's eyes widened and her jaw dropped as she took it in. There, on the cover, was a drawing of a young girl standing alone in the middle of a village facing off against a giant, malevolent looking elephant.

Back on the ship, Serenity was flipping through the book for the tenth time. "How many times are you going to go through that book. You can't read it." Kang-Dae mused.

"Amir told me what it was about. Plus, there are pictures." Kang-Dae joined her on the bed laying his head on her shoulder.

"Why did the queen want you to have this?"

"I may have tried to scare her into accepting our deal using my visions," she admitted with a hint of shame.

Kang-Dae lifted his head and stared at her incredulously. "What? I was desperate," she said defending her actions.

"Anyway, that word I said that night, 'echang' Amir says it's the name of a demon that takes the shape of an elephant. This story is about a group of villages that becomes terrorized by it. To appease it, they give it everything it asks for. But every time it returns, it wants more and more. And if they don't give in to it, it vows to destroy everyone. Eventually, one little girl convinces everyone and all the surrounding villages to stop giving in to him and fight back. Together they were able to cast him out."

"Interesting story," Knag-Dae said, flipping one of the pages.

"Su told Amir the book belonged to Prija when she was a child. I think my dream was meant specially for her. It was the only way she would believe me and want to help."

Kang-Dae lifted himself up, to look into her eyes. "You amaze me every day," he praised. A slow, shy smile spread across her face. She leaned over and pecked him on the lips. Kang-Dae's eyes darkened slightly and his eyes fell to her mouth. Suddenly nervous, Serenity turned her focus back on the book.

Amused by her shyness, Kang-Dae smirked. He threw himself in her lap, making her gasp. He pulled her arm to his chest and held it there.

"Tell me the story again." He demanded, closing his eyes and making her laugh.

CHAPTER THIRTY-TWO

Serenity opened the door to Kang-Dae's study. It was empty, but she knew it would be. After they returned from their trip, he'd been busy. Everyone had been waiting eagerly for his return to get his help and input on various things. At the moment, he was off talking to Hui about some theft. She wanted to use his calendar to prepare for any other events or important days that might be coming up. After this Gi thing, she didn't want to have to deal with any other type of event for a while. She searched his shelves, but didn't find one. She went into his drawers. "Ha!" she exclaimed when she saw it. She looked over it and was surprised to see only one date marked. The last time she'd seen it there had been a lot more, realizing this was not the same calendar. She, moved to put it away, but stopped when she noticed what the marking said. One of the characters looked like the character for moon. Serenity realized this was where he marked the day for the blessed moon. She felt herself growing mournful as memories of that night resurfaced. Not wanting to head down that road of sorrow, she put it aside and pulled out what turned out to be the calendar she was looking for. She started looking at it; taking note of Gi's celebration day and another festival. Which, if memory served her, was held in the city by the citizens- a relief. When she was done, she went to put both calendars away, but stopped when she noticed something. Putting both calendars out on the table side by side, she examined each one carefully. The date marked for the blessed moon didn't look right. The marking placed the date much earlier than it had been. She started counting in her head trying to get her days right, but it still didn't add up. The calendar had the moon date three weeks before the night she tried to return. Her blood ran cold.

'This couldn't be right.' she did the math again, carefully counting up each day; trying to remember how many days she'd been in a depressed stupor. Even if she added a few extra days to account for her unreliable mental state, it didn't match up. Had they gone on the wrong day? The annoying emotion of hope began to rise once more, though she tried to fight it. She was just beginning to come to terms with everything. She didn't want to end up disappointed again. She did the math again, and again, and each time getting the same answer. She pulled out her old study book of common characters. As she originally thought, the character she was looking at was for the moon. A sickening feeling stirred inside her. This must have been a mistake. Kang-Dae must have gotten the dates mixed up.

'How?' she thought to herself. It was clearly marked. Her breathing picked up. She thought back to his behavior in those days- his avoidance, the guilty look in his eyes she mistook for sadness. His inability to look at her that night. Tears filled her eyes. "no," she whispered to herself shaking her head. She did the math again, this time trying to recall what happened on the real night of the blessed moon. A memory surfaced that shattered her heart. She remembered him kissing her under the moon, how he'd pushed her to the brink where she'd wanted to give herself to him completely. The moon had looked so beautiful that night, so much bigger and brighter than usual. She recalled how upset he'd been when he first saw her outside staring up at it, as if he were afraid of what she would see. Serenity began to feel nauseous. He'd lied to her. And the night she should have gone home, was the very night she'd realized she'd completely fallen for him.

Serenity walked back to her room in a daze. She didn't let anything show as she moved through the halls, not wanting to alarm her guard. She did her best to keep her emotions at bay until she could make it to her room. Once she was inside, she collapsed against the door. She wept silently on the floor in agony. She couldn't comprehend any of what she'd learned. How could she have been so wrong about someone? How could she allow herself to get fooled so badly? That nauseated feeling was growing within her. She feared she would throw up soon. She sat there crying, replaying every touching and meaningful moment they'd had together. They were false; meaningless- a front he put on to distract her and trap her in this place. She wanted to scream out, to rage; break everything in her sight. She wanted to confront him and demand an explanation. '*No,*' she thought to herself. She couldn't let him know she knew. If he was capable of such deception, she had no idea what else he was capable of. Was he her only deceiver? Had her mother-in-law and Jung-Soo known as well? What about Amoli? Was there no one she could trust? It was too much. She felt like she was going to implode. God help her, she couldn't do this. To be betrayed by someone she'd trusted so completely, the pain she was feeling was indescribable. Anger, hurt, confusion and regret rained heavily on her. She lay on the floor arms, around her knees. She wanted desperately for this to be a dream, a horrible one and soon she would wake up in

Kang-Dae's arms, comforted by that familiar warmth and safety she'd always felt with him. What was she going to do now? How was she meant to live with the one who almost destroyed her with his lies?

'I don't have to,' she realized. If he had lied to her about the moon, she knew it must still be her way home. This meant all she had to do, was find out when the next one was. Once she got the opportunity, she would go back on her own and escape. Pain and rage shifted, transforming into strong resolve. She was determined now. She will make her own way home, if only to get back at him for ever making her feel anything for him. As far as she was concerned, he was a wolf in sheep's clothing. He was the enemy she would keep close until the right time. She would harden her heart against him and purge whatever feelings she'd had. They meant nothing now. Her priority, as it always should have been, was to get back to her real family. Difficult as it was, she pulled herself up. She washed her face, doing her best not to look like she just had a breakdown. She had to go on as if everything was fine, as if nothing had changed. The thought of having to pretend and still show affection for that man made her fury blaze once more, but she would get through it for the sake of her family; she had to.

CHAPTER THIRTY-THREE

Kang-Dae sighed as yet another petitioner approached the throne. He'd been there for hours now, becoming irritated due to fatigue and frustration. Another cart had been stolen. This was the fourth theft. He had to hold off on any more shipments until they could catch the culprits. No one could figure out how they knew when and where the wagons would be. Serenity had been the one who'd chosen those villages. Now the people were fearful, thinking they would be the next target. They refused any more aid from her. He knew that had hurt and frustrated her, but she wouldn't talk to him about it.

He had wanted to spend time with Serenity today. She'd been so busy lately, immersing herself in planning for the Gi's house celebration and other things. She had gotten a strange and sudden need to put more effort into different projects. If it was what she wanted, he wouldn't object. He just wished she would also take some time for herself. He felt distant from her the past few days. He couldn't quite explain it, but she seemed odd. She still smiled and talked in her usual brazen manner, but something in her eyes was different. Kang-Dae had hoped to rectify this new distance by taking her out riding, but the line kept growing. He was tempted to send them all off, but decided against it and resigned himself to carrying out the day. Maybe they could spend the evening under the stars.

That plan was nixed when he returned to an empty room that evening. Was she planning another late night again? That would be four nights in a row. He tried to bury his disappointment in optimism by telling himself she was slowly accepting her role as a queen. He only wanted her to have more than just responsibility here. He wanted her to have happiness. He told himself over and over that if he could just make her happy his actions would not be so horrible.

Kang-Dae decided to go and find her. If he couldn't spend time with her any other way, he could at least work with her. On his way walking outside, he paused to see her just walking around. She didn't seem to have a destination; she was just walking with her head down. He stopped himself from rushing over to her. If she wanted time to herself, he'd accommodate her. It stung a bit, knowing she rather be on her own than with him after so many days with little interaction. He turned and went back inside.

"The Queen had invited those in the surrounding villages to the celebration," he heard a feminine voice say. He peered around the corner to see some servants walking together.

"I heard she and the King's captain went out to personally invite them. Kang-Dae's ears perked up at that. She had gone out with Jung-Soo? 'Seemed like Jung-Soo was spending more time with his wife than he was these days,' a bitter voice spoke in his head. His irritation returned

266

as he left to go to his study. If he was enduring another lonely night, he may as well get some work done.

***

"Is it working?" Jae-Hwa asked excitedly as she and her father arrived outside the palace walls beneath the tree.

"Patience, it'll take time before we see real results. Subtlety is key in this plan," The conspirator said.

"They're not together as much- it seems like a good time to push even more," Yoon spoke.

"We will. She's giving us all the stones we need to bury her. We just need to expose them to the King."

"Are you sure it will be enough? He has been so blind when it comes to her," Jae-Hwa said.

"The more they are apart, the easier it will be. Soon she'll fall right into the trap I've laid for her, and he will no longer be able to ignore her unworthiness as Queen."

CHAPTER THIRTY-FOUR

Kang-Dae's mood was sour. The lords were hounding him about the food thefts, his headaches had increased, and Serenity continued to evade him. He'd gotten to the point where he was asking his servants about his wife's whereabouts. The numerous times he heard she was off with Jung-Soo made his irritation rise even more. It didn't matter if Amoli was often with them. His wife was off with another man and he couldn't even get her to greet him in the morning. He sat in his study most days, thinking of every report brought back to him. He wondered if this was his punishment for his deception. Was he being forced to watch her slip away from him, after doing what he had done to keep her there? His vision began to blur from the pain in his head. He rubbed his eyes aggressively. The council was meeting soon, and he'd see them both there. He dreaded what he might notice.

Jung-Soo and Serenity entered separately to his relief. She gave him a regular greeting with no special affection that he could see. The meeting began with Yu informing everyone that refugees were fleeing from the lands Katsuo had invaded. "They want land and provisions to live here while their homes are occupied."

"We do not have anything to spare," Yoon said.

"We can give them land and, with what we've gathered from Kah Mah, we can spare enough to get them started," Serenity spoke up.

"That stock must last. We cannot waste it on peasants."

"Those *peasants* are who help keep you fed," Serenity gritted.

Yoon scoffed. "And if we run out of food to feed our soldiers, will they fight in their place?"

"You don't mind using our resources for your little celebration, but this is frivolous to you?" Serenity retorted full of fire, a fire he had missed.

"What do you know? You have only been in our land for a few months. Ever since you've come, we've dealt with more thefts, deaths, and misfortune than we have ever had." Serenity rolled her eyes and shook her head.

"I'm sure it looks that way to a small-minded man like you," she quipped.

"My Queen," Amir spoke trying to calm the situation.

"You know nothing about this country or the way we do things. The only reason you are not just another peasant like those refugees is because the King is too bl-," whatever he was going to say next ended because he was suddenly in the air. Yoon yelped as Kang-Dae held him up by his robes. Yoon stammered and pulled at Kang-Dae's hands. Kang-

Dae threw him to the ground. There were gasps and exclaims from all around the room, but Kang-Dae didn't shift his focus from the man currently trying to scramble away from him. He pursued the panicking Yoon, unable to feel anything but rage. It consumed him. Yoon stammered out an apology, but Kang-Dae had no interest in it. He was out for vengeance- retribution, blood.

"Save your apologies. I'll take them out in your skin." Yoon paled and got to his knees bowling submissively.

"Please, my King. I'm sorry." Kang-Dae pulled him up by his clothes and brought him to his face.

"I grow tired of your apologies," he growled.

"Kang-Dae!" Serenity's sharp voice cut through the fog of fury he found himself in. "Enough. This isn't helping anything," she scolded him. Her words shamed him and the disgusted look on her face- a disgust for him- hurt. He threw

Yoon down and stormed off, unable to take anymore, leaving everyone utterly perplexed.

Jung-Soo was worried about Kang-Dae. His behavior was almost out of control. He was suddenly violent, quick to anger, and paranoid. He'd never seen him act in such a way before. He assumed he and Serenity were at odds, as she too had been acting odd whenever he mentioned Kang-Dae. He had tried to bring up his worries with her, but she just dismissed him. "Maybe he's always been this way and you're just now noticing," she said so callously it stunned him. Jung-Soo had no idea what was going on between the two, but knew it was serious. Even so, he wasn't so sure that their marital issues were the main cause of Kang-Dae's increasingly alarming behavior. Kang-Dae may be out of sorts when it came to Serenity, but never to this extreme. Even the way he had been treating him lately was alarming. He was cold to him, almost treating him like he was the enemy. This was beyond a little anger at putting Serenity in a dangerous position. No, this was something different. Only he had no idea what he had done to warrant such treatment from his oldest friend.

***

Serenity tossed in her sleep as she dreamt.

Kang-Dae struggled to find his way out of the green fog. He searched frantically for an opening, but everywhere he turned more fog would appear. The fog seemed to be tormenting him. He was covering his ears and shouting as if it was all too loud. Different voices were screaming at him from all directions. In the mist, there were three figures watching him. The fog began to enter his nose, mouth, and ears. He tried to block it, but it just crept its way inside his head until his eyes glowed green. He went still- limp. Suddenly, the figure behind him raised his hand and Knag-Dae mimicked the movement. The figure to the right did the same and Kang-Dae repeated the action, while tears ran down his face.

Serenity woke up curled up on her side of the bed, as close to the edge as she could get. She looked over and saw he was still asleep. Her first instinct was to wake him and tell him her dream, but she stopped. Why should she? This just might be the consequence of his actions. He didn't die in the dream or look close to death. Though he had hurt her like no other, she didn't wish him dead. Besides, this could be the distraction she needed to escape when the time came. Until she figured out what the dream meant she would keep it to herself. If something happened, she would deal with it then. That part of her that tragically still cared about him annoyed her. It would creep up on her every now and then, and speak to that naive part of her that would sometimes want to come up with possible excuses for him. But what he'd done was inexcusable. At the end of the day, he just didn't want her to leave. On the surface, that may have been sweet. But his actions essentially made her a prisoner, no matter how she looked at it. Although she wouldn't actively move against him, she decided she no longer had to help him anymore either. Let him feel some of the heartache he made her feel.

CHAPTER THIRTY-FIVE

Hui stood nervously before the King, along with Kyril and Satori. "We have not made any progress in finding the thief. Perhaps if we were to ask the Queen-," Kang-Dae's gaze shot over to Hui who stopped talking immediately.

"My King, we need to assume that whoever may have taken the poisons have the intention of using it. We need to take precautions with your meals,"

"Just *my* meals?" Kang-Dae asked his tone threatening. Satori swallowed, knowing he needed to tread carefully.

"Of course, I mean the Queen as well. Shall we inform her?"

"She's on her way out of the palace," Kyril spoke up. Kang-Dae turned toward him.

"What? Why"

"She's accompanying a shipment for the children, my King."

"Is Jung-Soo with her?"

"Of course, my King," Kyril reported, thinking it would relieve Kang-Dae.

Kang-Dae's jaw clenched. "Why?"

"Well, she insisted. She said he's good at keeping the children in line."

Kang-Dae's head began to pound once more.

"My King, about the theft," Hui started. "We can't rule out someone close to you could be planning something nefarious."

'Someone close to you.' 'She's with Jung-Soo.' Those words were swirling through his mind along with the way brown eyes that used to greet him so warmly were now cold and cautious. Kang-Dae stood up.

"My King?" Hui called out as Kang-Dae ignored him and left.

He made it to the gates just as she was about to depart. A surprised Jung-Soo watched him from his horse. Serenity's guards' eyes followed him as well. Ignoring them all, Kang-Dae stormed over to her carriage and tossed open the door, startling both Serenity and Amoli who were seated inside. "Come out."

"What are you doing?" Serenity demanded.

"Out!"

Amoli climbed out first. Serenity sat back stubbornly.

"I will not allow this carriage to move. You can stay in there all night or come out now," he warned. Serenity scoffed before coming out, refusing his hand as he tried to help her down.

"What is your problem?"

"There have been several thefts of our shipments in the past few weeks. Now is not the time for you to be going out."

"The kids are counting on me. If I don't get this to them, who knows what they'll do to get their next meal."

"I will send some men out secretly to do so. It is well known where and how you handle giving. You're just making yourself a target."

"How do you know it won't get stolen from them?" She challenged.

"I will make sure every precaution is taken."

"If you send a bunch of soldiers, you're going to scare them off and they won't come back. I need to be there, they trust me," she told him.

'Why don't you trust me?' he thought, too fearful of her answer to say it out loud.

"Until we catch these bandits this is how it has to be. No more shipments will go out."

"The shipments for the north are going out tomorrow!"

"Not anymore. We can't risk losing any more of our resources to our enemies." Kang-Dae maintained.

Serenity huffed. "Fine," she mumbled pushing past him.

Head low, he stood there feeling guilty. Even though there was truth in his words, he knew it was his jealousy that prompted his actions. When he looked up, the maids, soldiers, and nobles quickly averted their gaze. Was he becoming as much of a joke in their eyes as he felt?

***

Storming into the palace, Serenity almost bumped into Kyril. "Apologies, my queen"

"It was my fault," she muttered, too upset to look up.

"What is it?"

"The shipment north has been canceled."

Kyril tilted his head. "That is interesting, considering they have already left."

Serenity's head shot toward Kyril who was sporting a mischievous smirk.

"Really?"

"I was feeling a bit antsy, so I moved up the timetable. I was just about to report it to the King."

Serenity felt relieved, but a little worried as well. As angry with him as she was, Kang-Dae did had valid points.

Noticing her conflict Kyril asked, "Do you want me to call them back? I assure you they have more than enough men to handle any situation. Satori and Amir will take the northeast, while Nasim and Yu take the west. They are quite capable, I promise." Kyril assured. Serenity wasn't as sure as he was, but she trusted his word. Besides, the people needed food. They couldn't keep waiting.

"Don't bring them back and give it another day before you tell him" she said. Kyril nodded with a smile.

"Do not worry, my Queen. It will all work out and when it does, the King will be pleased." Serenity doubted it, but she didn't argue. At least some good would come out of today.

CHAPTER THIRTY-SIX

Serenity was starting to make moves. She was ready to go. Between Kang-Dae's betrayal and his mood swings, she was becoming convinced she might have fallen for someone dangerous. His behavior had become almost frightening. He barely slept in the room anymore, which she was partly grateful. But that annoying part of herself couldn't help worrying over him.

Serenity went to one of the scholars on her own, feigning a curiosity on the moon. She casually asked about the blessed moon. Having recently done the predictions for one, they were able to quickly come up with an answer; not only for the next one, but the next four. The closest was three weeks away, and then another a month after. She didn't have much time to plan her exit without Kang-Dae realizing what she was up to. The hardest part would be leaving the palace without suspicion. She would come up with some way. She would not be stopped this time.

Shouts from the throne room startled her as she walked by.

"Get them back here, now!" Serenity could hear Kang-Dae bellow. Jung-Soo stood outside his face stoic as usual, but there was concern in his stare. She could hear Kang-Dae yelling some more through the door, but she couldn't make out the words. Jung-Soo looked to her as if to say, 'are you going to do something?' But she turned and walked away. She refused to get involved. She saw the flash of disappointment in his eyes. Nevertheless she continued, even as the need to intervene attempted to come forth. As far as she was concerned, that was no longer her business.

She locked herself in her study, pulling out her map. She crossed off another route. She'd been trying to find the best way to the lake. The more research, she did the more she found not all the routes were very safe. A knock at the door had her yelling at the interrupter to leave her alone. Arezoo's strong voice penetrated the door.

"My Queen, I need to speak with you." Releasing a frustrated sigh, Serenity put the map away. She unlocked the door and moved aside to let Arezoo in. The other two stayed outside.

"What is it?" Serenity asked.

"I need to know what you are planning," Arezoo stated bluntly. Serenity stiffened.

"What?"

"My Queen, you have been secretive. The King is not acting like himself. The two of you are not behaving as you once did."

Serenity stayed quiet. "That time when you were "ill" for days, you wouldn't leave your room. It was after you were supposed to visit family. That was not meant to be a trip you expected to return from, was it?"

Serenity shifted her weight looking down. "When I became captain of your guard, I decided to serve you. You are my Queen. Whatever you need of me, you can ask. I do not want you attempting whatever this is alone."

Serenity chewed on her bottom lip. She trusted Arezoo to protect her, but she didn't know if she could trust her to let her go. If she didn't take this chance, she could lose her opportunity. Then again, maybe God was sending her a guardian angel.

"I need to go home," she stated. Arezoo gave no outward reaction.

"What do you need me to do?"

***

Satori was at the head, leading his men. He was far behind Amir, but he wouldn't alter his pace. He didn't want them to be an obvious target. He had begun to regret agreeing to this plan the moment he set out. He didn't know why he'd listened to Kyril. To demand they leave early without warning as well. The man was incompetent.

"Sir!" One of his men raced up to him a note in hand. "Word just came from the palace. We're being ordered back by the king." Satori's brow furrowed. 'Why would he order them back now when they were so close to their destination? Had Kyril sent them out without his knowledge?' Incensed Satori ordered his men to turn around. He never should have trusted him.

"Sir, what about Lord Amir, shouldn't we tell him?" Satori stared down at the letter than to the north.

"No." Amir was another one who held the Queen in such high regard. Let him complete her foolish demands. When it is over, it will be Amir who has to answer to the

King. Satori and his men set off for the palace without looking back.

CHAPTER THIRTY-SEVEN

Amir ordered his troop to keep watch along the

river. This was their second stop on their route across the

north. The people had been given word to make it to one of

these destinations for provisions and food. A large group

had come out, much larger than the first. They had already

given out more than half of what they had brought. People

were disappointed by how little it was. many voiced their

disappointment, but there was nothing he could do. Amir

made sure to ration what was left for the next stop. It was

taking longer than it should have, since Satori had never

shown up. Amir should not have been surprised by his

actions. He supposed he had given him too much credit in

thinking he cared more for the people than his own ego.

Knowing they had been stationed there too long, Amir

announced that they would be leaving soon. There were

more shouts of disagreement, but Amir didn't entertain

them. He couldn't make them accept that they were doing the best they could. The people were hungry and lived under constant fear of attack. A little food wasn't going to appease them so easily.

"Enemy spotted!" The shout came from behind. By the time Amir looked, his heart seized as a force of men in armor came through the trees. The people screamed and scrambled away only for another group to come out from the other side and block their escape.

"Protect the people!" Amir ordered his men. They were very clearly outnumbered, but he couldn't let the people die. He could at least give them a chance to escape. His men took position between the enemy and the civilians. "Give no mercy!" Amir shouted and his men shouted their agreement. The enemy charged and Amir braced for the impact.

CHAPTER THIRTY-EIGHT

The celebration looked to be going well. Many people had attended. The Gi family possibly being put out by those they consider beneath them being in attendance was only the icing Serenity's petty cake. She wanted the people who were having a hard time to be included in the palace's events. They deserved it as much as them. Maybe it would help them see those in the palace as people and not faceless dictators. She busied herself by mingling with the noble houses and commoners. Arezoo, Nasreen, and Gyrui were always by her side just in case.

Amoli had returned just in time for the event, which Serenity was glad for. Serenity made sure Amoli understood she was not on duty and should enjoy the celebration as her guests. Amoli had been very uncomfortable with the idea but became excited when they were dressing up. Serenity had a special dress made for her. Her eyes had lit up when she saw the formal 2-piece fuchsia gown with gold decals and a sheer matching robe. Serenity had fun making her up and doing her hair for a change. When they entered the hall, Serenity noticed Amoli's eyes immediately searching for someone. Serenity hid her smile, knowing exactly who that was. Deciding to help her friend out, she led her through the crowd to search for him.

She walked straight past Kang-Dae, who was being bombarded with the many lords and ladies of the land. That was perfect for her, she didn't have to have an excuse to stay away. Her attempts at keeping things as they previously were was practically impossible. Every time she had to fake a smile or laugh, she wanted to strangle him. She thought it easier just avoiding him altogether. Lady Gi was giving her the stink eye from across the crowd, but she could care less. She had way bigger issues than one woman's jealousy. Not to mention, at this point, she wanted to tell the woman the title and King were up for grabs as far as she was concerned.

Once she found her opening, she would be leaving both behind.

Kang-Dae politely answered questions, listened to bad attempts at jokes, and repeatedly declined requests for frivolous things he had no interest in. He just wanted the night to be over- not that he had anything to look forward to afterward. He would find no solace from Serenity. What he had at first dismissed as overexcitement in her new role, he now began to think was something else. Now, he suspected she was purposely finding reasons to avoid him. He thought maybe it was just her still trying to cope with her loss, but now he wasn't so sure. He wanted to spend time with her to help her through it, but she seemed determined not to. If they did speak, it was only to argue.

They hadn't even arrived at the celebration together. She'd left earlier in the day, claiming she wanted to help Amoli get ready. When she did arrive, he hoped she'd at least take a moment to join him. But he was instantly disheartened when she had walked past him. He lost sight of her after Lord Pei had pulled him aside. His eyes searched around for her and he finally spotted her with Amoli, conversing with someone. She was laughing. The sight lightened his heart. Despite the tension between them, he still liked to see her happy. As the person shifted, he saw that it was Jung-Soo they were talking to. He appeared to be the one making her smile. It should have made him happy, but a trace of bitterness began to form once again. She looked so genuine. He realized that was what had been missing the past few days with her. Sincerity. She had been putting on a false persona with him, but with Jung-Soo she seemed completely unburdened. He could feel his face fall.

"My King," Lady Gi approached him. He didn't take his eyes off Serenity and Jung-Soo. "This was such a wonderful event. I hoped you would thank the Queen for me." He gave her a distracted yes. She continued, seemingly oblivious to his darkening mood.

"She worked very hard. I was worried she'd worked too hard honestly. I was glad she had the captain of the guard to help her." He looked at her then.

"He did?"

"Oh yes. The lady said he was very eager to keep her from being overwhelmed. He is such a dedicated man," She said with a sly smile. Kang-Dae looked back at the two, missing the mischievous glint in Jae-Hwa's eyes as she watched him. Kang-Dae couldn't stop staring at them now. He noticed how relaxed she seemed and how uncharacteristically open Jung-Soo was. Yoon's words suddenly came back to him about their unique relationship. Just how unique was it?

Laughter and music filled the room, but Kang-Dae wasn't affected by any of it. His mind was being haunted by unwanted thoughts. Lord Pei was speaking to him, but he was not listening; just wordlessly nodding every so often to feign interest. Kyril was suddenly at his side encouraging the older lord to give his "brilliant" suggestions to Satori. Lord Pei seemed a bit disappointed but agreed. Kyril turned to face Kang-Dae. He didn't say anything, he just stared at him. Kang-Dae felt uncomfortable under his scrutiny. Suddenly, Kyril put an arm around his shoulder and began leading him away.

"My King, do not force yourself. You don't have to stay. Your presence has been noted. You- should go rest." Kyril's suggestion was tempting, but he couldn't leave. As if reading his mind Kyril continued, "The queen has her guard with her, and no one will dare touch her with so many in attendance. Besides Jung-Soo will not leave her side." Just hearing his name sparked something deep and dark inside him.

"No," he said sharply. Kyril looked taken back by his tone. Kang-Dae cleared his throat. "I will stay," he told him. Kyril's worried expression deepened, but he conceded to

Kang-Dae's wishes. "Well, let us go watch the performers in the courtyard." Kang-Dae wasn't very interested until Kyril mentioned Serenity had already headed that way. Agreeing, the two walked outside together.

The people awed at the different performers. The firebreather was the most popular, having drawn dozens over to him. The woman performing her dance with the silk scarves had drawn several of the men's attention. In the back, a shadow puppet show had begun intriguing all the children in attendance, many of whom were the one's Serenity had regularly gone out to meet on her excursions outside the palace. Watching the different classes of people intermingle and enjoy the night had started to lighten Kang-Dae's mood.

"My King, this way; you don't want to miss this," Kyril assured him. They walked over to a small stage. A man and woman were performing a scene. The woman's face was caked in make-up and her clothes were ill-fitting. The man kept fumbling over his words and looking out to the audience. "This troop is one of the worst in the city." Kang-Dae made a face.

"Then why would I want to see it?"

"We're not here to watch them, we're here to watch that," Kyril pointed to Yoon who was glowering in the corner. Kang-Dae felt a genuine smile fill his face.

"I suppose you had a hand in this."

Kyril brought his thumb and index finger close together making him laugh. His attention was brought back to the bumbling couple on stage. The man was wailing as the woman flounced around in a ridiculous amount of jewelry.

"What is this?" Kang-Dae said with a cringe.

"It's an old play, and the only one they know," Kyril chuckled. "About a duke who thinks he's lucky enough to find the perfect wife. He was so mesmerized by her beauty, he didn't notice all the misfortune she caused him and everything he was losing until he was left with nothing."

"I thought it might be a reminder of the trouble you avoided by not marrying Lady Gi," Kyril joked.

Kang-Dae smiled, but it didn't reach his eyes. The story before him was starting to feel familiar, and not because of Jae-Hwa. His eyes searched across the courtyard, finding Serenity once more- still with Jung-Soo. They were watching a balancing act. Serenity's eyes were wide and her mouth hung open in awe. Her beauty was captivating, and a dark feeling formed in him. His eyes turned back to the stage. People laughed as the man foolishly offered his wife a priceless gem, which she snatched from his hands happily.

How often had people warned him about Serenity? How often had he dismissed them because he'd convinced himself they were the foolish ones; that she was harmless, that she needed his protection? He thought back to his life before that fateful day when he'd stumbled upon her at the lake. His life had not been perfect by any means, but he didn't recall going through this much heartache... this much trouble. Suddenly, the laughter around him felt louder. Only they weren't laughing at the fool on stage, they were laughing at him.

CHAPTER THIRTY-NINE

Serenity was practically running to the healing

room, not caring how she looked. Her guard kept formation

around her as she moved and poor Amoli did her best to

keep up. By the time Serenity entered the room, Kang-Dae,

Kyril, and Satori we're already there standing over the

prone man on the bed. They looked up at her as she

answered. Serenity's hands flew to her mouth at the sight of

a bloody and bruised Amir. "Is he?"

"He's still alive, my Queen," Kyril answered,

feeling her with immense relief.

"What happened? How did they know they were

there?" She asked.

"We do not know, my Queen. They were

outnumbered and ill-prepared to face a force of that

magnitude. Many of his men that ventured out with him did

not return. There are reports that there were some civilian casualties as well." Serenity felt her stomach turn. Her eyes drifted to Satori.

"Where were you?!" She demanded. For the first time ever, he looked ashamed as he lowered his gaze. "You were supposed to be there with him. If you had, maybe we wouldn't have lost so many!"

Satori was uncharacteristically silent, keeping his head down.

"Do not place your guilt on him," the hard voice of Kang-Dae sliced through the room, shocking everyone.

"What?" She turned to him with a frown.

"I told you the shipment should not go on. I warned you it was too big of a risk and you purposely ignored me. This is the result. You share just as much blame in what happened."

Serenity was struck silent. What could she say? Yes, Satori's action may have cost lives, but her decision definitely did. Those people- those soldiers, they would still be alive had she not attempted this in the first place. Tears she'd held back for Amir flowed freely for her grief and guilt.

"My Queen," Kyril spoke walking over to her. "Let me escort you back. There's nothing more you can do here." Unable to do anything but obey, she allowed Kyril to lead her away. Once they reached the hall, Kyril spoke. "Do not worry. I will speak to him, tell him this was my doing. You should not blame yourself. Sometimes, no matter how much we plan, things cannot be accounted for. We will pay Katsuo back 100-fold for this," Kyril promised, but Serenity was too focused on the lives lost. How stupid was she? She had been playing at this queen thing. It was easy to hand out food and keep nobles satisfied. She had forgotten that her decisions could cost people their lives. Today was a horrible wake up call. The sooner she left the better. She was no Queen. Just two more weeks and she could leave all this behind.

CHAPTER FORTY

Both the council and the nobleman and women of the court sat before Kang-Dae in the throne room. Serenity had not come, which Kang-Dae was grateful for. She shouldn't be here for this.

"My King, the people are rightfully upset. They were promised protection and now things are worse for them."

"I understand their anger. It was an unfortunate event, and we are doing our best to remedy it."

"With respect, my King, I do not think there is much to be done. With the occupancy in the north, any moves we make to help will lead to war; a war we still are not prepared for."

"What do you suggest?" Kang-Dae asked.

"Perhaps if the Queen were to make a statement of apology-,"

"Why?!"

Kang-Dae's sudden shout made the men flinch. "My King, it's been rumored that the Queen was the one to sanction this mission. Therefore, its failure-," The lord started.

"Its failure is due to Katsuo's plotting and nothing more," interjected Kang-Dae.

"My King, I wouldn't dare say such a thing," the man backpedaled. He looked over to his men who put something in his hand. The lord unrolled a scroll and showed it to Kang-Dae. He jumped out of his chair and snatched it up. It was a crude drawing of Serenity that featured the words "unworthy" above.

"These were found in the inner city." Kang-Dae tossed the offensive thing to the ground.

"The Queen is not going to apologize. I want everyone caught with those brought straight to me," Kang-Dae ordered.

"Yes, my King, but what shall we do about the north?" Kang-Dae contemplated looking at the ground before raising his gaze once more.

"We're not prepared for a full war right now, but we have enough men to organize an evacuation. We can get as many people out as we can to bring them further inland. I'll need the northern lords to help."

"Of course, my King."

"We will begin as soon as we can gather the men."

***

Kang-Dae stormed through the palace. He left everyone in the throne room unable to stand the sight of any of them anymore. If he didn't, he feared he would kill one of them. Seeing how quickly the people could turn against Serenity after all she tried to do infuriated him. He'd been rightfully angry hearing about what she'd done behind his back, but he understood her reasoning. She wanted to help the people. His anger at her came from his own fears of how the people would react and it was disheartening to know he was right.

"My King," a soft voice called to him. Jae-Hwa was approaching, as always dressed in her best. Surprisingly, she wasn't with any other ladies of the court, or even her attendees which was rare. There was only her personal guard who trailed far behind her. He was going to keep walking, not caring to even pretend to be polite, but she stood in front of him effectively blocking his path.

"My King, how are you?"

"Fine." He tried to walk again, but she moved to stop him again.

"Forgive my candor, but you seem as though you carry a great weight upon your shoulders. It's been so long since I've seen you smile. It saddens me to see you this way."

He wanted to shout he didn't care. Her concern was not what he wanted. "If you would like, you can visit with me anytime. Maybe I can help," She spoke innocently enough, but the look in her eyes promised different things. The idea of even touching her put him off. He didn't want her or anyone else but his wife, even if she didn't want him.

"No." He pushed past this time only to feel her hand boldly on his arm. "My King, I only want what is best for you and our country. It's clear that you no longer hold the Queen's affections. A crumbling marriage brings forth a crumbling kingdom. If you are rethinking your match-," he snatched his hand away, outraged not just at her, but the possible truth in her words. 'Everyone could see it,' he thought. 'Her affections for me have left her. Now, she gives them all to Jung-Soo.' He thought back to the other night, how he'd attempted to touch her shoulder as she slept, only for her to recoil from him. Even in her slumber, she wanted nothing to do with him. Every day she showed how little she cared for him, but he couldn't stop wanting her. Maybe she had enchanted him.

"My King," Jae-Hwa's voice pulled him from his thoughts. "I know it may be hard for you to see the truth. But it's better that you see it now before any more damage is done."

Kang-Dae shut his eyes, trying to hold back his anger. "Get away from me," he spoke slowly.

"Please, my King," Jae-Hwa begged, grabbing his arm once more, holding it tightly in her dainty hands.

"Everyone sees it- how much you care. Can you honestly say she feels the same, even now?" Kang-Dae's temper flared. "I have you loved since I came here. The day I arrived, you were there."

9 years ago

Jae-Hwa couldn't control her racing heart as the carriage slowed to a stop. Not only would she be reuniting with her father after so many years apart, but she would be meeting the prince as well. Her father told her so many great things about the prince in his letters, describing him as a brave up and coming warrior and confident young man. He told her all about his early success in battle and his mischievous antics around the castle, which amused the Queen and frustrated the King.

Jae-Hwa kept going over all her lessons in her head. Her father had made it clear that when she was there, she should carry herself as a perfect woman of nobility and grace. The carriage door opened, and she stepped out into her new home. The size and majesty of it almost overwhelmed her. It was more beautiful than she'd imagined. A man stood waiting in front of her. "Your father has asked me to show you where you will be residing" Though she was disappointed her father wasn't there to receive her, she hid it well beneath a smile she'd perfected when she was 13. "Thank you." The man led her and her servants through the grounds. It was a lot to take in. She feared she'd get lost if she ever ventured out alone. The sound of cheering and loud chatter drew her attention. She turned to her left to see a group of men cheering as they watched two men fight in the grass. At first, Jae-Hwa feared something was wrong, but realized from the smiles and merriment of the men around them, that this must be a sport of some sort. The men held onto one another trying to make the other fall. She couldn't see their faces, but the taller one appeared to be winning. Jae-Hwa's pace slowed when the *taller one finally brought the shorter one down. The men cheered as the taller one stood. Jae-Hwa was shocked by how young he looked. With a victorious smile, he raised his arms triumphantly. He was handsome, very handsome. His shoulder-length hair was all mussed and wild. The young man helped his opponent up. He had a more serious look on his face, but he didn't seem upset over his loss. The taller one threw his arm over his shoulder and laughed. The sound made her smile. Suddenly, he turned her way and she couldn't move. At that moment she knew he was the prince, the future king, and her future husband. He smiled right at her and she felt her cheeks go red. Shyly, she turned away too flustered to do anything else, as she rushed to keep up with the attendant.*

Jae-Hwa had kept that smile in her heart all these years. Even today, the memory of it brought her the same elation as she had back then.

"I always knew we were meant to rule together as one."

"I have no memory of that day," Kang-Dae responded coldly trying to pull away, but Jae-Hwa held onto him. "I know she has you confused, but I can help you. And once we are married the people will thrive once more-," Kang-Dae threw her off. Jae-Hwa lost her footing and fell. Her man raced over to help her.

"9 years ago, 5 years ago or 1, it doesn't matter. I've felt the same thing for you then as I do now. Nothing. Same thing I've felt for the dozens of ladies I've smiled at."

Jae-Hwa's sight began to blur as the tears appeared. "There has never been one moment that I considered you to be anything more to me. At most you had my respect as a lady. But seeing you this way- throwing yourself at a married man, I don't even have that for you." Jae-Hwa's chin trembled. "Understand this, Lady Gi, no matter what happens between me and my wife, I will never regard you as anything more than a pitiful tool of your father. I pray one day you will find a will of your own." The King cast her one last pitying look before walking away, to find the only woman who had his affection.

Jae-Hwa sat on the ground unable to do more than cry, as the King walked off leaving her shamed and heartbroken.

CHAPTER FORTY-ONE

Jung-Soo hunted Serenity down. He was becoming tired of being involved in their marriage, but once more he found himself intervening. How tragic that his new habit involved fixing the damaged relationship of his best friend and the woman he had fallen for. He found her in the practice room, sparring with her guard. He paused, momentarily stunned by her progress. While Arezoo was the obvious superior fighter, Serenity was doing surprisingly well for having only been training for such a short time. As he watched, he could see the determination in her. She had a focus that was admirable but worrying all the same. Snapping out of his thoughts he moved forward.

"Wait outside," he announced to her guard. All the women looked at him. They then looked to their Queen, unsure whether to follow his command or not. Serenity looked at him and he could tell she was upset that he had interrupted their session; probably wanted to tell the women to ignore him. Fortunately for him, she didn't fight him and told them to wait outside. Once they were gone, she continued to practice with her staff attempting to ignore him, but he knew she was listening. "You need to do something."

"I am doing something, you're just interrupting me," She snarked swinging her staff around.

"How long are you going to let this continue?"

"He's a grown man and a King. He could do whatever he wants."

She still had not looked his way. He knew it was her way of staying detached. Tired of the game, he yanked the staff from her hand. She glowered at him, but he had the attention he wanted.

"What happened?"

"Nothing."

"Do not lie. If your petty arguments cause the fall of the kingdom, I'll kill both of you. What happened?" She stood silently fuming. He could tell she wanted to say something, but there was a hint of distrust in her expression which bothered him. Since when had she had that look with him?

"It doesn't matter."

"If it is affecting him this way, it matters," countered Jung-Soo.

"I have nothing to do with that," she shrugged.

"Talk to him." She turned to walk away, but he stopped her with a hand on her arm. "Serenity," he said sincerely. She turned her head defiantly, but not before Jung-Soo saw the pain within her eyes. "Tell me."

She looked as though she wanted to cry. The door opened and Kang-Dae appeared. His gaze immediately landed on the both of them, looking at the intimate way Jung-

Soo was touching her. Without a word, Kang-Dae stormed over and pulled Jung-Soo away from her so hard he almost fell. They both stared at him.

"It's always you," he sneered at Jung-Soo. Not understanding his statement or his hostility, Jung-Soo could only stare. Kang-Dae took a threatening step toward him, but Jung-Soo stood his ground preparing himself for whatever came. "You're just like them. Using me to get what is mine."

"I don't know what you mean," Jung-Soo replied honestly.

"I should have left you in the street," Kang-Dae spat. The words were like a dagger in Jung-Soo's heart. This was not the Kang-Dae he knew.

"Get out of my sight." Jung-Soo didn't move. He glanced at Serenity. He did not want to leave her alone with him while he was in such a state. "Now you disobey me?"

He asked taking another step forward. "Maybe you wish to be King, as well. Shall we fight for the honor?"

Jung-Soo lowered his head, not out of fear, but in hopes of de-escalating the situation. "You will not take what is mine," Kang-Dae growled, taking another step only to be stopped. Jung-Soo looked up to see Serenity pulling him back. He spun around so aggressively Jung-Soo feared he would hurt her, so he quickly put himself between them. This action appeared to infuriate him more because he let out a growl and threw Jung-Soo to the ground. Serenity let out a loud gasp. Kang-Dae stood over him. There was genuine hatred in his stare that Jung-Soo could not understand. Kang-Dae stepped to him once more, this time it was Serenity who threw herself in front of him.

"Stop it! What's the matter with you?!" Kang-Dae's stare left Jung-Soo and turned to her. The was anger still there, but it was accompanied by longing as well.

"Come," he demanded. Jung-Soo stood up quickly to intervene once more only for Serenity to stop him.

"It's fine," she said, but there was an uncertainty in her voice. His heart clenched as Kang-Dae grabbed her by her hand and pulled her out of the room.

Serenity barely kept up with his fast pace as he continued pulling her through the halls. She wouldn't admit it out loud, but she was scared of him. He barely resembled the man she fell for.

"My King, My King!" Amir called out, stopping Kang-Dae's- march to her relief.

"What?!" he snapped, stopping Amir in his tracks. He lowered his eyes before reporting they received word that Katsuo himself has been seen in the marshlands. Kang-Dae slowly released her arm and she stepped away. "Gather everyone to the hall." Amir bowed and ran off. Kang-Dae turned to her, now that the anger was gone there was remorse in his eyes. But Serenity wanted nothing to do with it or him. Turning on her heels she walked away. That night she slept in her old room.

***

She dreamed she was trapped in darkness. There was no trace of light anywhere. She kept moving, hoping at some point she'd reach the end. She could hear the sound of rushing water. She ran toward it, knowing it could lead her to her destination. Then a low whistle sounded, and something struck her. Serenity didn't know what it was, but it pushed her back. She was hit again and again, getting weaker with every blow. In the darkness, she heard the screams of her comrades as they too were hit. She tried hard to stay standing, but she was hit once more- this time in the head. Her neck snapped back, and she fell backward.

CHAPTER FORTY-TWO

"It's a trap," Jung-Soo concluded.

"We don't know that for sure," spoke Yu.

"Are you doubting our Queen?" Jung-Soo asked, voice low. Kang-Dae hated how offended he was on Serenity's behalf.

"Of course not. But it is possible the vision may not be what she thinks it is. After all, there have been missteps in the past," Yu said.

"That had nothing to do with her visions," Jung-Soo growled, looking pointedly at Satori who had the decency to look away.

"It's not something we should take lightly," Amir said.

"It was more than a warning though. I think the sound of the river was a clue. It might be where a large portion of his army is," Serenity theorized.

"The only river close to the marshes is the Pen Nai. The only area large enough to hold an army of this size would be the plains. We can be there in 3 days," proposed Amir.

"You're still recovering, Amir." Serenity reminded him.

Amir shook off her concern. "I am capable of leading my men, my Queen. I want the chance to take as many men from Katsuo as he has taken from us," he said head high, a hard look on his young face.

"Perhaps we should send a small troop to investigate the marshes as well. Jung-Soo and I could lead them," Kyril offered. 'Now even Kyril was beginning to doubt her,' Kang-Dae noticed.

"You could very well be going to your deaths," Nasim spoke.

"Why take the risk? Vision or not, you know the information is questionable at best. We've never seen a single report about Katsuo himself appearing anywhere, now we suddenly know exactly where he is," Serenity continued. "How can we risk you and Jung-Soo's lives on an unknown?" Kang-Dae's hand fisted at his side hearing Jung-Soo's name come out of her mouth.

"My Queen," Kyril began.

"No, we're not doing that," she stated.

"That's not your decision," Kang-Dae spoke coldly. Her eyes flashed to his, quickly filling with fury.

"I thought it was both of ours," she argued.

"My Queen, this is the best way. If your vision is right, we will find out the truth of it. Trust in us. We will not let you down," Kyril assured her.

Kang-Dae considered everything that had been said.

"I could go on my own, my Queen," Kyril continued. "Jung-Soo can stay behind." Kang-Dae glanced over at Jung-Soo standing by his wife.

"Jung-Soo will lead a small group to Sang. Move at night, off the roads. Report back what you see." The look of utter disbelief and anger on her face almost made him take back his words but he did not.

"No, he won't," she spoke nostrils flaring.

"My Queen, it's alright," Jung-Soo tried to calm her an action which only infuriated him more.

"No, it's not. This is a ridiculous and stupid risk that's not worth your life."

"Leave by nightfall," Kang-Dae ordered. Jung-Soo bowed.

"Then I'm going with you." both Kang-Dae and Jung-Soo look up alarmed.

"My Queen, you cannot," Kyril said.

"It's my vision, so it's my responsibility. I should be the one to go."

"You will not!" Kang-Dae declared. Serenity didn't even look at him.

"If he goes, so do I," she vowed. Face red, Kang-Dae called for his guards. Everyone in the room couldn't believe what was happening in front of them.

"Escort the queen to her chamber and keep her there," he growled. The men did as they were told and went over to Serenity.

Infuriated, she cursed at him. As she was led out of the room, she whispered something to Jung-Soo as she passed, which only intensified his aggravation.

Jae-Hwa sat amongst her tattered dresses and scattered jewelry. The scissors in her hand rested as she stared blankly at the painting of her mother. After her humiliating attempt at the King, she'd returned to her room. The first thing she saw was the new dress her father had brought her hanging on the dressing partition. 'Fit for a queen,' her father said when he gave it to her. It was what he always said every time he gifted her with anything. Everything she had was fit for a queen. Everything that she learned had been taught to her, so she could be a queen. Everything that she was had been contingent on the fact that she would be queen. But she was not queen, and she never would be. The realization that her dream had only ever been that, broke something inside her. With an anguished cry, she grabbed her scissors from her vanity and tore at the offending gown, ripping it to shreds until it was nothing but a pile of scraps. When she was done, she targeted the rest of her gowns, unable to stand the sight of them anymore. She'd spent her life being molded into the perfect queen- what was she if not that?

CHAPTER FORTY-THREE

The moon illuminated their path, but not by much.

Jung-Soo crept slowly between the trees. 'Listen for the whistle. Come back.' Serenity's whispered warning from that day in the war chamber echoed in his mind. His heart thudded more than usual, but he remained calm. He listened out for the sounds of the forest, but he heard none- not even the chirp of insects. His heart rate picked up even more. He motioned for his men to be still and continued to listen. He stood unmoving as the seconds turned to minutes. Still nothing, but he could not relax. Something wasn't right. He debated whether to go further into the darkness to search out anything unusual. It was his orders to check out the area, but he knew it would be a mistake. Serenity was right, this was a foolish endeavor. He gave the sign to retreat. They would go back for the night and scope out the area in daylight.

Moving with the stealth of a lion they retraced their footsteps to head back to their hidden rendezvous.

It was low at first, so low Jung-Soo wasn't sure he'd heard it, but then it came again much clearer: a whistle.

"Down!" He shouted out just as a flaming arrow flew by, barely missing him as he dropped to the ground. A slew of arrows followed suit, hitting the trees and ground around them. "Move!" Jung-Soo ordered. Jung-Soo knew whoever was out there couldn't see them and must only have an idea of where they were. How they got the information, he didn't know; but that was tomorrow's problem. Right now, he had to get his men out. The fire was spreading around, blocking their previous path. The man to his left cried out. He looked to see an arrow sticking out of his leg. Jung-Soo and another quickly patted the fire out to keep it from spreading. They each took an arm and carried the man through the onslaught of arrows. They moved as quickly as they could while his men surrounded them using their shields and bodies to block any possible arrows. Arrows began to rain heavier on the left forcing them to go right. Then they were heavier in front forcing them to go back. They were being herded, yet they had no choice but to keep moving. 'Come back,' Serenity's plea almost cried out in his mind. He tightened his hold on his man and kept moving. They were forced into the road, a clear target.

"Break off!" He ordered. They had a better chance if they scattered. His men hesitated not wanting to leave their captain.

"Go!"

The men ran off leaving him with his injured man and the other soldier. They began moving towards the woods. Another arrow whizzed past them, though it seemed like the number of them had lessened considerably. They kept on moving.

"Leave me," the man pleaded.

"Quiet!" Jung-Soo snapped. They moved through the trees, using them for cover. The three men came to a stop. Coming out from the darkness were men in black armor, with bows and arrows pointed directly at them. Jung-Soo stared them down as his heart pounded. He raised his head high, ready to meet death if need be. Putting the injured man fully in the other soldier's hold he grabbed his sword. The men began to laugh. Jung-Soo smirked. "You should turn around." The men laughed harder only to stop short when two men fell forward- dead, arrows sticking out of their backs. The men swiftly spun around just as another group of arrows came out of the darkness hitting them all.

Jung-Soo lowered his sword. Nasim and a group of her soldiers came out.

"Did you get them all?" Jung-Soo asked.

"If we did not, I'm sure our King will."

Jung-Soo was surprised to hear that Kang-Dae had to come himself. A few months ago, he would have expected it. But given the state of their relationship lately, he honestly hadn't anticipated it.

2 days earlier

Jung-Soo closed up his pack. He was about to head down to the gate to follow Kang-Dae's orders when something slipped under his door. It was a small scroll. Picking it up and unraveling it, he recognized the King's handwriting immediately.

'Take your men through the south part of the marshes. Make your presence known. Nasim will come from the north once the enemy shows their face.'

Jung-Soo was more than a little relieved. Perhaps he still cared after all.

Jung-Soo and his comrades made their way back to the road where the rest of Nasim and the King's soldiers were rounding up Katsuo's surrendering men.

Kang-Dae turned toward him, cleaning the blood from his sword. "We need to move if we want to make it in time. Kyril and Amir are already there. If we are late, Katsuo will have the upper hand." Jung-Soo quickly mounted a horse.

They rode out that night as the sun rose. Jung-Soo and Kang-Dae were at the lead. It was almost a day's ride from where they were, so they had to hurry. As they came up to the plains, Kang-Dae turned to speak to Jung-Soo.

"I will take the left," Jung-Soo said before Kang-Dae could tell him to do that very thing. Jung-Soo raced away with his men following behind. Kang-Dae chuckled lightly before leading his men right.

Katsuo's men were charging. Kyril and Amir's men were outnumbered by several 100, but not one hesitated to charge forward to meet them head-on. Katsuo's soldiers pressed on confidently, eager for victory. By the time they noticed Kang-Dae and Jung-Soo coming from the sides, they didn't have time to defend against them. Their men moved through their lines easily, barreling through with their horses. One, two- five men fell with a swing of Kang-Dae's sword. Katsuo's soldiers either ran or joined the many fallen. By now, Kyril and Amir had joined in surrounding them on three sides.

Jung-Soo was off his horse taking on two opponents at once. Kang-Dae quickly dismounted and joined him. They fought back-to-back as they had done many times before. Neither gave the enemy any opening, constantly surprising them by swiftly switching positions. The sudden change in fighting styles threw them off, giving both Kang-Dae and Jung-Soo an opportunity to neutralize each of them. Kang-

Dae gave Jung-Soo a once over making sure he was alright as Jung-Soo did the same. Once both men were assured the other was alright, they went right back into the fight.

The battle didn't last much longer. Those who didn't fall ran. The Xianians cheered in victory. Kang-Dae slapped Jung-Soo jovially on the back. This was much needed. He hadn't had anything to celebrate in weeks.

***

Serenity and Arezoo looked over the map together. Even though Kang-Dae had ordered his men to keep her inside the room, she was still allowed to have her guard with her. So, she'd demanded Arezoo be let in. This was a good chance to form a plan for the next night of the blessed moon. It was less than a week away.

"Once they notice we're gone, he's going to know what our destination is. The main road won't be viable," Arezoo speculated. "We need a route that will get us there in a short amount of time, but also isn't accessible to a large party."

Serenity pointed at the map. "Through these hills?" Serenity suggested.

"Not a good option when traveling at night."

Chewing on her lip, Serenity thought hard. They didn't have many options. Her eyes fell to a small line on the map.

"Do you think you can get a boat?"

"A boat?"

"If we leave through the east gate, we can make it to this stream. We can place it there beforehand." Serenity followed the stream on the map with her finger. "It flows right by these hills. By then it should be daytime and easier to make our way through before sunset."

"That's possible." Arezoo agreed.

Serenity's anxiety about the upcoming night was beginning to ease, but there was something else that filled her with tension.

"Arezoo, what are you going to do after I'm gone? They might blame you." Speaking it out loud made the truth of it that much more real to Serenity. When she brought Arezoo in on her plan, she hadn't stopped to think about how it could affect her. She was Captain of the Queen's guard. If something happened to Serenity, she might be the first to be blamed.

"I will be fine, my Queen," she said without a trace of doubt or worry.

"Arezoo, maybe you should stay behind. They'll just think I ran away on my own,"

"No."

"Arezoo."

"As long as you are here, you are still my queen and it is my duty to protect you, no matter the risk to me," she affirmed. "Do not worry over me. I will simply say I followed after you once I noticed you missing and failed to stop you in time."

Serenity was still unsure about it all, but from the determined expression on her face, made it clear she wouldn't be changing her mind.

Feeling a bit emotional, Serenity hugged the female from the side. Arezoo didn't move to pull away or hug back, letting her have her moment. "Thank you," she said softly.

"You're welcome, my Queen."

CHAPTER FORTY-FOUR

Instead of returning home, Kang-Dae had the men set up camp for the night allowing them a chance to celebrate. Kang-Dae watched amused, as his men drank and joked with one another. He still had some men posted in case any of Katsuo's men felt like returning. He didn't drink, preferring to keep himself sober-minded. Jung-Soo was off on his own, keeping watch. It wasn't surprising for him to keep out of the festivities, but there was a heaviness weighing on him that was not normal. He'd be lying to himself if he said it was the first time he noticed it. Guilt filled him as he knew he was the cause. The anger and suspicion he'd been feeling towards his oldest friend dimmed as he recalled how they fought together side by side, like they had numerous times before. He was moving before he could come up with a reason not to.

Kang-Dae offered Jung-Soo a drink, a simple gesture. He declined as Kang-Dae suspected he would, but getting him to accept the drink was not the goal.

"Katsuo will think twice before trying anything else." Jung-Soo gave the smallest of nods. "You and the men can have some time off. Not all at once of course, but every one of them should be able to spend some time with their families; even if it's for a short while."

"I will tell them," Jung-Soo said.

"You as well."

"I have no family to visit." Jung-Soo reminded him, and the statement stung. Not long ago, he would have said Kang-Dae was his family. Now, it seemed he no longer felt that way. Kang-Dae knew he had no one to blame but himself.

Jung-Soo turned to him and stared as if he were waiting for something. Kang-Dae looked away and began to walk off.

"Will you really not speak of it?" Jung-Soo asked. Kang-Dae stopped. He would've liked to pretend he had no idea what Jung-Soo was talking about, but he did. Jung-Soo continued to watch him daring him to speak up.

When Kang-Dae continued to stay silent, Jung-Soo lightly scoffed and began to walk off.

"You love her." It was not a question nor an accusation, just a statement of fact. Jung-Soo froze in his tracks. Kang-Dae was unsure he would ever turn around, but he slowly faced him, meeting his gaze.

"Voicing it makes no difference. Nothing has or will change." He said it as if it was so simple. The dark anger he'd been battling was trying to creep up once more, but Kang-Dae didn't want to entertain it. "Did you think it

343

would?" Jung-Soo asked. He sounded offended. Once again that guilt ate at him. Jung-Soo had always been his most trusted advisor, his most loyal soldier, and his closest friend. Looking back on the past few weeks, it was hard to pinpoint when and why he'd allowed himself to doubt him.

"I do not know," he finally answered honestly. "It's been different. She's been different." 'With me' he added on still unable to voice it out loud.

"So have you." Kang-Dae had to pause. 'Had he?' He knew he'd been more short-tempered lately, but it had always seemed justified... at least at the time. Now, looking back after being away from it all for several days, those moments seemed foggy and hard to understand.

"You should speak to her. There's something between you two, neither of you want to talk about it and it is slowly destroying you both. Don't let it."

It sounded good. One simple conversation, everything could return to normal. The truth would be out and the never-ending guilt he'd been feeling might finally be appeased. But it wasn't that easy. His confession wouldn't end their issues, only compound them. In the end, he'd lose more than her affection. It was unthinkable. "This is my punishment," he said aloud before he could stop himself. Jung-Soo's brows crinkled.

"What?"

Kang-Dae shook his head and started to leave, but Jung-Soo was quick to block his path. "Why would you think that?"

"Leave it," Kang-Dae said attempting to walk away once more, but Jung-Soo remained in his way.

"What did you do?" That guilt increased tenfold.

"Let me go," he growled needing to get away before it consumed him.

"Say it."

"Stop."

"Say it!"

"It was the only way!" He screamed, pushing Jung-Soo away. "It was the only thing I could do. I couldn't let her go." Jung-Soo's confused expression slowly shifted from shock to disbelief until finally the implication of his words penetrated his mind, and the horrified look that appeared last tore at Kang-Dae's heart.

Jung-Soo shook his head in disbelief. "No. You would not do that. You'd never purposely break your vow." Kang-Dae couldn't look at him any longer.

"I had no choice,' he said softly.

The silence between them was unbearable. That overwhelming, horrible shame was pounding on him in light of his confession.

"She has to know."

"No."

"Kang-Dae!" It was the first time he had ever risen his voice at him.

"I can't."

"You must."

"Do you want her gone? Do you want to lose her forever?" Kang-Dae demanded.

"It's not about what we want," Jung-Soo said. "How can you disregard your vow for your own selfish desires?"

"She'll die!" Jung-Soo took a step back like he'd been struck. "If she goes back, she will not survive it." Jung-Soo searched his face trying to confirm the truth in his eyes.

"Are you certain?"

"I'm not willing to risk it," Kang-Dae told him. Jung-Soo's head dropped as he tried to process what he'd been told. He rubbed his hand through his hair, exasperated. He turned back to Kang-Dae.

"Why lie?"

"You know why," Kang-Dae said. Jung-Soo knew as he did that Serenity wouldn't let anything stop her. She'd refused to just take the word of others. Nothing would have dissuaded her from returning. "I can lose her to her world and her family. It would have killed me to let her go, but I would have done it for her because it's what she wanted. But I cannot let her go to her death. That I will not do." The nightmare he'd had all those weeks ago still haunted him.

Serenity was in a black dress standing on the edge of a cliff waving at him happily. He was trying to reach her- to warn her, but she just smiled at him telling him everything would be alright. She turned around to step off. Kang-Dae ran for her, desperate to catch her. His fingers managed to grasp at her dress, but she slipped through his fingers and went over the ledge. Kang-Dae screamed as he watched her

fall. At first, she seemed at peace, but before she could hit

the water it became a dark black hole. Her face filled with

panic and fear as she called out to him for help, but he could

only watch helplessly as she was swallowed by the darkness.

After that dream, Kang-Dae knew he had to make a hard decision.

Jung-Soo looked as conflicted as he had felt before he made that decision. "It is not right."

"Maybe, but there's no alternative. Even if we were to tell her and by some miracle she agreed to stay, she could never live happily here. The guilt of choosing her life over her family's peace would eat at her every day. This way, this way she can be blameless. She can have comfort in the fact that she had no control over it."

Even in the darkness, Kang-Dae could feel Jung-Soo's judgment on him. Kang-Dae wished he would condemn him, rage at him, tell him he was a dishonorable man. It's what he'd been telling himself ever since he made that choice. Somehow, being the only one to condemn himself made it seem worse.

Saying nothing, Jung-Soo turned his back on him and walked away. It hurt, but nothing could make him feel any worse than he already did. The weight of his decision was always there pressing on him, reminding him of what he had done to her. Even in their precious moments, he could never fully allow himself to feel joy, refusing to forget what he'd taken from her. Her well-being was all that mattered. He had been willing to put on the mask forever to give her the blissful life she deserved to make it up to her. But in his heart, he knew it would never be enough.

CHAPTER FORTY-FIVE

When they arrived back at the palace, Kang-Dae
didn't bother going to see Serenity. He already knew she
wouldn't see him, not with the way they'd left things. It
was one of those decisions that had made sense at the time.
But now that his anger was gone, he'd realized he'd gone
too far. Instead, he went straight to his study, choosing to
spend another night there until he could work up the nerve
to apologize- and he knew had much to apologize for. He
fell asleep at his desk, his lantern burning through the night.

***

Yoon went to visit Jae-Hwa as he had not heard
from or seen her in days. He thought maybe she was busy
with her part of their plan. She had been subtly planting
doubts about the witch in different ears, allowing the roots
of distrust to take hold. She still was not aware of the other

things he and their cohort had done to ensure their plan's success, but it was for her own good.

"Jae-Hwa," he called out before entering her room. The first thing he noticed was how bare it looked. All the beautiful decorations and artwork had been removed. "Jae-Hwa!" he called out once more.

Movement from his left drew his attention. He turned to greet her, but his words died in his mouth. His daughter was not his daughter, not the one he'd raised. The girl he'd brought up would never be seen in such a state. Dressed in a grey dress with a plain white overlay, the outfit was almost indistinguishable from what the servants wore. Her hair was not in any type of style, only left to hang loosely to her waist. She wore no jewelry or makeup.

"Jae-Hwa," Yoon gasped out, not understanding what he was seeing. "What is this? Why are you dressed this way?"

"I had to borrow this from Asha. I had nothing left to wear."

"What happened to your clothes. Did someone take them?" he asked becoming angry.

"I threw them all away. I don't need them anymore." She said in a calm, low voice. Yoon shook his head in confusion.

"What do you mean?"

"Those dresses were for someone else, not me. I am not a queen, and I never will be," she explained.

Yoon made his way to her taking her into his arms.

"My beautiful girl, don't despair. We are making progress every day. The people have already begun to turn against her, and the King has started to distrust her. It won't be long until he's at your feet begging-," Jae-Hwa pulled away with a huff.

"Stop it, father! None of it's real. I was never going to be queen. It was a fantasy- a story you told me that I foolishly believed."

"Where is this coming from?" Yoon asked, never hearing her speak in such a way.

"From a place of truth, something we should have faced long ago," Jae-Hwa told him. Not liking her tone or what she was saying, he decided to give her some time to herself. When he returned, they could talk again, and he would remind her what they were working toward.

"I will get some new dresses. You cannot be seen like this," he told her, not wanting her to embarrass herself or him.

"It is fine for where I'm going."

"Going? Where are you going?"

"Yenoa, home."

"Jae-Hwa don't be foolish, we're this close to our goal."

"No father, we aren't," she said dejectedly. Eyes downcast and shoulder slouched, she walked away, no longer carrying herself the same.

Yoon's temper flared. Now his daughter had given up. She was no longer the bright and beautiful girl he knew. This would not stand. He needed to speed things along. He would show her that nothing could stand in the way of their destiny.

CHAPTER FORTY-SIX

When Kang-Dae awoke still at his desk, his head was pounding so bad it hurt to open his eyes. He needed to see Hui, to get something to dull the pain. He practically stumbled down the halls, the pain making it hard to walk straight. Someone was suddenly at his side helping him along the way. They arrived after what felt like hours and he collapsed into a chair. He vaguely heard Hui asking him something. He muttered about the pain in his head as the darkness crept on him. A strong scent hit his nostrils. The more he inhaled it the more the pain began to subside, and his vision returned.

"Is that better, my King?" Hui asked. Kang-Dae nodded.

"Has it ever been this bad?" he asked.

Kang-Dae shook his head.

"It's worrying that you've been suffering this for so long. With that poison thief still on the loose, I don't think it's something we should ignore."

"No one has poisoned me," Kang-Dae slurred a bit, the medicine affecting his speech.

"My King, until we catch them we can't know for sure. Whoever did it could have access to you the average person does not." Yoon spoke. Kang-Dae looked over at him, surprised that it had been him that had brought him to Hui.

"If someone were poisoning me, they are doing a poor job of it," Kang-Dae said, rubbing at his eyes.

"They may want to do it slowly, to relieve suspicion. Back when Kah Mah had two rulers, the queen ended up slowly poisoning the king so the people would think he was only getting sick. It could be the same thing." Hui sucked in a breath as Kang-Dae tensed.

Yoon, realizing what he said tried to rectify it. "I don't mean this is the same situation, My King. I know the Queen would not poison you."

All Kang-Dae heard was 'queen', 'poison', 'you" echoing in his mind. Suddenly, he couldn't stop thinking of how Serenity had been the only one spotted outside this very room before the theft took place; how her eyes were now always filled with disdain whenever she looked at him; the way she never allowed him to touch her anymore; how she preferred Jung-Soo's company to his. It had all seemed so ridiculous before, but now, now it made so much sense it was alarming.

"Where is she?" he asked in a low voice.

"I do not know my King, perhaps Jung-Soo would-," Kang-Dae tossed the table in front of him and it went flying into the wall, breaking into pieces. Hui and Yoon took a step back. Kang-Dae didn't say another word as he stormed out of the room, only one destination in his mind.

***

Jung-Soo avoided Serenity. He was too afraid he'd confess everything to her. Though a part of him knew she should be told, like Kang-Dae, he feared what it would mean. He tried to clear his head with training. The feel of the staff in his hand making life so much simpler for him. He should have known fate loved to mess with him when Serenity entered.

"You weren't even going to let me know you were alive?" she asked.

"I am alive," he informed her, putting away his staff while refusing to look her way.

"You know how scared I was?"

"You didn't need to be. The King had it all planned out. I was never in danger," he admitted.

"What do you mean?"

"Kang-Dae knows someone in the council is talking- giving away important information. He couldn't make his plan public," Jung-Soo explained.

"He could have told me," She said, clearly offended over being kept in the dark.

"Could he?"

"What's that supposed to mean?"

"With the way you've been treating him, are you surprised he no longer comes to you?" She rolled her eyes.

"So what, he's the one who shouldn't trust me?" she scoffed. The way she said it had Jung-Soo staring at her closely.

"What do you mean by that?"

Serenity pressed her lips together and looked away.

"I'm glad you're okay," she said before making a hasty exit.

Serenity walked out of the sparring room and ran right into Kang-Dae. Still angry at him for having her locked up in her room like a child, she moved to walk past him, but he blocked her path. She moved to the other side, but he did again. "Let me through," she said through gritted teeth.

"I need to speak with you," he said.

"I don't want to speak with you," she replied, once again trying to walk around him only for him to grab onto her arm.

"That hurts," she huffed, trying to pull her arm free.

"I said we need to talk." Serenity didn't know when Jung-Soo had come out, but suddenly he was there pulling Kang-Dae off her and placing her behind him. The look in

Kang-Dae's eye was frightful. The last time she'd seen it was when he had almost killed Su.

"I think you should calm yourself," Jung-Soo suggested warily, but Kang-Dae seemed past the point where for words.

As if to prove it, Kang-Dae reached out, grabbed Jung-Soo by the head, and slammed it into the wall making Serenity scream out. Jung-Soo fell to the floor in a daze, blood dripping from his head. Serenity's guards stepped up and Kang-Dae turned those cold eyes to them. Not wanting them to get hurt, she rushed to him. "We can talk," she said keeping her voice as steady as possible.

"My Queen," Arezoo harshly called out.

"It's okay, stand down. We're just going to talk." As Kang-Dae grabbed her hand and pulled her along, she turned back to see Nasreen helping Jung-Soo to his feet. As

Kang-Dae pulled her further and further away, all she could do was pray.

CHAPTER FORTY-SEVEN

Serenity was dragged to the bedroom, his grip on her painfully tight. Her heart raced with uncertainty and fear. She was horrified to see his treatment of Jung-Soo. She put herself between him and her guards because on some crazy level, she still believed he wouldn't hurt her. But as he pulled her into the room practically throwing her inside, she suddenly wasn't so sure. He slammed the door shut so hard the walls rattled. Her heart pounded as he stared at her, his fierce expression still present. He stepped toward her and she stepped back. He paused, a flash of sadness appearing on his face. For a second, he reminded her of the old Kang-Dae. But just as quickly as it came, it passed and the fury returned. Once again, he came at her. This time he moved quickly, not allowing her time to escape. He grabbed her by her arms and moved to kiss her. Serenity turned her head to avoid him. He released her with the curse.

"Would you prefer if I brought Jung-Soo? Is he the only one worthy of your affections now?" She folded her arms and gave him the side-eye. "What? Now you won't even speak to me?" He bent down to her level. "Do you wish to kill me?" He asked. She turned to him with confused eyes. "The poison thief, was it you? You want to get rid of me and be with him?" Serenity was starting to believe he was losing his mind.

"What are you talking about?"

"You think I do not see. That the people do not see? They're all laughing at me while you and he flaunt yourselves around the palace." Deciding she'd had enough, she tried to walk away from him only for him to pull her back.

"Has this been your plan from the start? To take my kingdom, my captain, my life?" Serenity pulled herself from his grasp.

"You are acting crazy."

"You show me a taste of your love only to deny me over and over, and I am crazy?" He laughed dryly. "Tell me, have you laid with him yet? Have you let him touch you… kiss you?!" he asked, becoming more and more aggressive with every question.

"No! You're being ridiculous. Nothing like that has ever happened."

"Why should I believe you? You hide yourself from me. You keep secrets. Why should I believe anything you have to say? Since your arrival, my life has known no peace. I once thought you to be a blessing, now I see you for the curse you are."

His words shouldn't hurt. They should not have bothered her because she should not feel anything for him anymore. But it did.

"Go to hell," She spat trying to leave.

"I'm already there, can't you see? How could I not have seen you for what you are?" The way he was looking at her hurt and she became angry because of it; angry at him and angry at herself for allowing it.

"I asked myself the same question when I found out what you did." Kang-Dae froze.

"You talk about not believing me when you have been lying to me this whole time. What? Did you think you could hide your dirt for me? I am a seer, remember?" There was a moment, a brief moment, when she could see him come through once more. He was hidden beneath the guilty look on his face. She could see the Kang-Dae who sat with her when she took the arrow for him; the one who had apologized so sincerely when she'd been poisoned. Kang-Dae shook his head and he disappeared once again, in his place was the unstable doppelganger.

"You should be grateful." The audacity of his words left her speechless. "You have no idea what I've done for you."

"Done for me? You lied to me, imprisoned me here, and tried to keep me from my family!"

"Is that why you wish me dead? Is that why you cling to Jung-Soo? Did your hate for me drive you to him?" Too outraged and tired she gave in to the anger needing to hurt him.

"Yes! Yes, I hate you!" She spat. He went deathly quiet, looking distraught at her words. "I despise you!" She lied.

"Stop."

"You disgust me!"

"Enough!"

"I want to destroy everything you love, so you can feel how I felt. I want to kill you with my own hands and live the rest of my days with Jun-," his hands reached out to grab her and she ducked out the way, running for the door, but the heaviness of her clothes slowed her. He caught her from behind. She threw her head back hitting his chin. He grunted and his grip loosened enough for her to slip out. Running for the door again she managed to open it a little before it was slammed back shut. Kang-Dae tossed her from the door. She landed on her shoulder with a whimper. He was on her before she could recover, pushing her onto her back. His were eyes frighteningly empty. His hand trailed up her arm slowly, tracing over her bruising shoulder. Serenity panted, fear keeping her still. His hands lingered over her collarbone before making their way to her throat. As soon as she realized his intention, she tried to scream out for help, but her cry was cut off by his hand around her neck.

Serenity grabbed at it trying to pull him off her as his grip tightened, closing off her air supply. She hit him, scratched him desperately trying to stop him. Her eyes began to water as she tried to take in air, a horrible feeling of deja vu filled her. As she stared into his eyes, she saw nothing of the man she first met- the man she fell for. *He's not in there,* she thought as her vision began to dim. As her hands began to go limp, his face shifted. Tears sprang to his eyes and he released her. She scrambled back gasping for air, taking in as much as she could.

"I'm sorry," he whispered. Tears streaming down his cheeks. "I'm sorry." She wanted to run, but was still trying to recover. He crawled over to her, and she tensed up in fear. He simply lay his head in her lap, hugging her at the waist.

"It's alright," he whispered. "You can kill me. I will let you. I will die if it's what you want," he cried. She stared down, too horrified to say anything. "Just let me be with you a little longer. Just a little longer, then you can kill me."

Serenity struggled to swallow as the urge to weep came upon her. Her conflicted emotions were just as bad as his conflicted personalities. Jung-Soo had been right, something was terribly wrong with him. She'd been too consumed with her pain and anger to see it. She raised a shaking hand to his head tentatively sweeping the hair off his neck as he cried. Through her watery eyes, she saw something that made her pause. On the back of his neck, she could see the line of his veins, but what made her feel sick was the fact that they had a green tint to them. The same green she'd seen him fighting to escape in her dream. Her eyes widened in horror.

CHAPTER FORTY-EIGHT

Serenity continued to comfort and soothe Kang-Dae until she could coax him to sleep. As he slept, she watched him, feeling guilty at what he must be suffering. Perhaps if she had said something when she first had her dream things would not have gotten this bad. With everything that happened, she found it impossible to hold onto the anger she had. He had clearly been tormented. In a moment of clarity, she allowed herself to remember who Kang-Dae was; how he'd been her rescuer when she'd first arrived. The lengths he went through to keep her safe- not trapped, just safe. He cared for her, that much she knew. Despite his lies, she knew he was a good man. She could not allow him to suffer this way. Trying not to wake him, she carefully slid out from under him. She looked back at him as she headed toward the door, hoping he would stay asleep until her return.

Once she left the room, she ran into her guard, all three sporting equally concerned expressions. Arezoo's eyes darkened as she took in the bruise forming around her neck. "I'm okay," she assured them. She looked to Arezoo and Nasreen. "I need you to guard the door. Don't let anyone in." She commanded. The women were clearly confused but agreed. "Gyrui, find Amoli, tell her to meet me in the medicine room." Gyrui nodded and ran off.

Serenity practically ran there. Everyone she ran past stared as the queen made her way through the grounds. She entered the medicine room. Hui was there, giving her his patented sneer of distrust, which she ignored. She went past him in search of Mehdi who was in the back. Talking slowly in Xianian, pausing only a couple of times to get the wording right, she asked, "Is there anything that can cause someone's blood to turn green?" Mehdi didn't appear to understand her. She sighed in frustration. Trying once more, she pointed to a vein in her arm, emphasizing the word green. His eyes shifted a bit before they widened in understanding.

He pointed to his head and spoke the word for pain. Serenity nodded. Mehdi raced to the shelf and began searching for something. Amoli arrived soon after. Her eyes widened as she took in Serenity's mussed state. After a few moments, Mehdi returned with a book. Flipping through the pages he stopped once he found what he was looking for. Showing her a picture of a small plant, he explained in Xianian what it was and Amoli began translating. "Omgi, very dangerous. Some believe it can be used to curse others into doing their bidding. It taints the mind, making the person more agreeable to suggestions."

"Is it fatal?" she asked fearfully. Mehdi shook his head.

"No, but some have gone mad when exposed to it for too long."

A sudden gasp escaped Amoli, drawing everyone's attention.

"What is it?" Serenity asked.

"Ah-Mei," Amoli said, her voice growing sad "She had always been so happy. Those last few days before," Amoli broke off unable to finish. "She wasn't the same. She used to be able to ignore what the overseer would say about her, but suddenly she started believing everything that she said- no matter how untrue. Maybe what happened with her, had something to do with what happened to the King." Realization dawned on Serenity as she processed Amoli's words.

"But why were only those two affected? It can't be the food," Serenity speculated out loud.

Mehdi shook his head and spoke, Amoli was quick to translate. "It has to be inhaled. For it to have such a physical presence in his blood, he had to have been subjected to it for weeks."

"Inhaled?" Serenity repeated, wondering how they could have pulled that off.

Deciding she would have to worry about that later, she chose to focus on eliminating the toxin.

"What's the antidote?"

"There isn't one." Serenity's heart clenched.

"There's nothing we can do?" she asked not wanting to believe it. Mehdi thought for a moment before speaking.

"It may be possible to burn it out of him," Amoli translated.

"What does that mean?" Serenity asked.

Mehdi left once more to retrieve something. When he returned, he had a blue vial in his hands. "Two drops of this will cause a strong fever. He will have to be watched carefully. If it gets too high, it could become fatal."

Serenity was hesitant to grab it after hearing that. She didn't want to risk his life trying to save him, but what choice did she have. He could not go on like this. As she reached for it, a hand came and snatched the vial away from Mehdi.

"Are you insane?" Hui exclaimed. "I will not allow you to poison our King."

"Give it to me," Serenity demanded not raising her voice.

"No. You are nothing but a blasphemous witch whose very presence has caused nothing but chaos and discord within this place. You may think you have our King fooled, but the people have begun to see you for the godless heathen you are."

"I am far from godless and I can assure you I need no spells or magic to deal with you. I am going to save the King.

If you try to stop me, I swear to the God I serve I will personally introduce you to whatever god you want." Serenity meant every word, and Hui must have seen that because he didn't struggle when she snatched the vial from him.

She looked back at Amoli. "Bring the rest of the King's guard to our room."

CHAPTER FORTY-NINE

Serenity poured Kang-Dae some water. He seemed much more clear-headed after his rest, but Serenity wouldn't be fooled into thinking he was fine. She'd already coated the cup with the serum Mehdi provided as well as mixing small amounts of valerian root essence to help keep him in an unconscious state, hoping to make this as painless as possible for him. Mehdi made it clear that the toxin would need at least two days to fully burn out of his system. Kang-Dae accepted the cup without hesitation. His trust in her even in the midst of his madness made her feel even more guilty.

"Stay with me," he asked holding on to her hand. She nodded and helped him lay back down, curling herself into his arms. He wrapped her up, holding her as close as he could. He was asleep only after a few minutes. Once she was sure he was out, she stepped out to see both her and his guard outside their room. "No one but Amoli and Mehdi is allowed in, no matter what," She told them. They vocalized their understanding.

"You three will watch during the day and the King's guard will relieve you at nights."

For this to work she couldn't have anyone trying to stop her. She would take care of him by herself. No one could know what they were doing. The culprits could not catch on. Serenity had already had Gyrui watching Hui carefully to make sure he didn't talk. She sent word to her mother-in-law so she wouldn't worry too much. And as far as the council knew, the couple was spending much needed time alone together until further notice.

Arezoo pulled Serenity to the side, away from the others. "My Queen, you are meant to leave tomorrow. If you do not, you'll miss your chance," Arezoo reminded her. Serenity looked toward the door.

"There will be other chances. I can't leave him now, not like this." Arezoo nodded and rejoined the others.

Serenity went back inside and sat at the edge of the bed watching him. 'I'm sorry. I'm going to fix this.'

The fever started around midnight. His skin was only slightly warm. He stayed asleep to her relief. She didn't sleep at all that night, too paranoid about the possible side effects of the drug. Mehdi had warned her about the consequences if the fever got too high, including seizures. So, she was effectively terrified. She would not be taking her eyes off of him. By the time his skin was practically ablaze, she stayed no less than a foot away from him. She spent hours cleaning the sweat from his drenched body while force-feeding him enough water to keep him alive.

By day two, her body urged her to sleep, but she didn't dare. She changed his clothes for the third time, not wanting him to get a cold on top of everything else. She vaguely heard someone outside the door trying to get in to speak with him, but her guard was effective in keeping them out and sending them on their way. When Amoli brought food, she only ate enough to keep herself strong. She fed him broth and water. The delirium started soon after that. He would speak things in his sleep. Most of it didn't make sense, but sometimes he would speak words of apology which tugged at her heart. That night her worst fears manifested when he began to seize. She could do nothing but fruitlessly try to cool him down with water and the small amount of ice she had. For one terrifying second, she thought he'd stopped breathing. Her relief was great when he finally calmed, and his breathing returned to normal. She spent the next few hours with her head on his chest just to make sure his heart continued to beat.

Serenity once again wiped his brow as he continued to toss and turn, mumbling her name. She shushed him, hoping to soothe him. "It's okay, I'm right here." She reached for the cup of water on the table by the bed. She prompted him to take the sip. He only took a couple before collapsing back into his pillow. She couldn't stand seeing him like this. Despite everything, she didn't want to see him in pain. But she knew she had to suck it up or he could die, and she could not allow that.

Kang-Dae started muttering incoherently. Serenity stroked his hair. Serenity shushed him once more not sure what he was saying. "I'm sorry, my Neeco," He whispered in Xianian.

"Just rest," she told him, dismissing what she assumed was an apology for their fight earlier.

"I just wanted to save you. I did not want to lose you." Serenity froze. "Won't let you end up like them." Serenity's brows furrowed in confusion. 'What was he talking about?'

"End up like who?" She asked.

"You won't be like them. Won't let you. Save you."

"Save me from what?" She pressed.

"Min warned me ..."'" he muttered before descending into incoherent gibberish. Then he went still, fast asleep. Serenity sat there staring down at him. 'What was that about?' At first, she thought he was just feeling guilty over his treatment of her, but now she realized he might be apologizing for lying to her. And from the sound of it, there was a major piece of the story she was missing. Could there be a reason for his treachery, a reason that went beyond what she'd initially thought?

Once the night passed and the fever broke, Serenity was finally able to relax. She thanked God that it was over and Kang-Dae appeared fine. He was still sleeping, but he looked better and the green tint in his veins was gone. She was bone-tired having had little to no sleep in several days, but she couldn't rest yet. She washed up and dressed. She called in Amoli to sit with him for a bit. The young woman saw how tired she was and pleaded with her to rest first, but Serenity felt this could not wait.

"Where did Ah Mei spend a lot of time? Was it any place where the King could have been?" She asked Amoli.

"She cleaned his study for him, many times alone."

Serenity left her guard behind as she moved toward her destination. In Kang-Dae's study, it was dark, the lanterns had yet to be lit. She started searching around, trying to see if there was anything unusual. According to Mehdi, the toxin was inhaled. So, it had to be somewhere he and only he spent a lot of time. 'What could he inhale that he wouldn't realize he was taking in?' she thought to herself. 'Would the smell not give it away?' Unless it was a smell he was used to, she realized. Her eyes fell onto the various lanterns around the room. She reached for the one at his desk.

She took it apart revealing the candle inside. It looked ordinary enough. She reached for the one hanging behind his desk and took it apart. She did the same to the one across the room, then another and another. Looking at the different candles, she didn't notice any abnormalities between them at first glance. She inspected each one carefully. It took a while before she saw it. There were specks of green in the candle from the desk. She examined every candle once more, but it was the only candle with such a defect. She reassembled each lantern replacing all the candles except for the tainted one. She placed a different candle in the lantern by the desk so as not to alarm the culprit. She hid the candle among her dress and went to see Mehdi.

The young apprentice confirmed the traces of the toxin within the candle. He claimed it was rare and hard to find. Whoever found it must have had the resources to afford such a thing. That didn't narrow down the list as much as she liked as all the council had those capabilities, though a couple stood out more than others. She went to Amoli next to ask her who was responsible for supplying the lanterns, but she didn't know. Serenity sat thinking about her dream, trying to force a vision for answers. She thought back to what she'd seen and what she might have heard. She recalled the smoke and the distraught look on Kang-Dae's face, but there was something else. He looked hurt almost betrayed. Could whoever have done this have been someone he trusted? She thought hard trying to remember anything else she may have overlooked when she had been too in her feelings to notice. She closed her eyes and begged God to help her recall the other part of her dream. She sat for hours not thinking of anything else. It came back in pieces, a glimpse here and there. One by one, she did her best to reconnect the dream. The two puppeteers came back to her slowly, but there was something else. Behind the figures was another person with a woman's silhouette. She was slowly backing away from the other two, each step causing a weight to drop off her until she was finally free to disappear. Just like that, she knew exactly who was involved and if she was. Serenity knew her father was a part of it as well. Serenity thought back to the betrayed look on Kang-Dae's face. She knew it meant the last culprit was someone she would not expect. She needed to root them out. Someone like that was far too dangerous.

CHAPTER FIFTY

Kang-Dae still felt groggy and tired, even though he had just woken up. His body felt weak, like he'd been fighting for days. He couldn't recall what had led to this feeling. Had he been sick? He felt something warm in his hand and turned his head with much effort. Serenity was asleep next to him holding his hand in hers. He tried to remember what happened. What could have occurred that led to this? He could only remember seeing Hui and feeling angry. Even those memories were foggy. It was as if he had been watching it from inside himself and not experiencing it. All his memories from the past few days felt like that. Serenity slept soundly next to him. He couldn't resist stroking her hair. It felt like forever since he touched her. He knew they couldn't continue on the way they had been. He needed to fix it, even if it meant admitting the truth. He didn't want to continue without her, but she was suffering, and their volatile relationship was starting to affect those around them. He couldn't let this go on. He pulled the blanket over her and kissed her cheek. Needing a bath, he left the room surprised to see Serenity's guard outside the door. They all bowed and greeted him. "What are you all doing here?"

"It was the Queen's orders," Arezoo told him. Confused, Kang-Dae decided he would get an explanation later.

Serenity slept over a day. Amoli informed Kang-Dae of his fever and how she had taken care of him the whole time. It felt good to know her concern for him was still there, but there was something in the way people stared at him now that unnerved him. Even Jung-Soo regarded him cautiously. He remembered his anger and frustration, but he had a hard time recalling why he had felt that way.

Kang-Dae was right there when Serenity opened her eyes, nervously awaiting what he would see in them when she looked up at him. The warmth he saw in them filled him with great relief and hope. "Hello," he greeted carefully. She gave him her sweet smile.

"Hi. How are you feeling?" She asked, eyes barely open.

"I feel good, better."

"Do you need anything?" She asked, even though she was the one who had just woken up after sleeping the day away.

"No. you should eat," he told her. She nodded tiredly and slowly got up. Seeing how bright it was, her eyes widen. She asked him how long she had been asleep and was surprised by the answer. He assured her it was fine, and nothing happened while she was out. But she looked a bit worried, asking if he spent time outside the room. Her relief when he answered, he said he'd only gone to bathe confused him.

"I've got to meet with the court," she told him as they ate.

"You don't have to do that today," he tried to convince her feeling she still needed to rest, but she declined; determined. He began to worry she was distancing herself again. Any reservations he still had disappeared when she kissed his cheeks as she left him. He went to grab his cup and his sleeves rolled up to reveal healing scratches. He didn't remember how they got in there.

***

Serenity found Yoon chatting with a couple of nobles in the courtyard. "Councilman Yoon?" The dirty look he gave her only increased her simmering anger, but she held it in. "Walk with me, please." She didn't wait for him to respond or object. She walked off, leading him away from the men and back towards the palace. She brought him to her study, making her guard stay outside. The annoyed look on the man's face, the way he dared to look as though he was being inconvenienced made Serenity want to slam his head into the wall. Once alone, Serenity dropped all pretenses and allowed him to see the full extent of her anger. Taking her dagger in hand, she slammed the man into the stacks while covering his mouth to keep him from shouting. Yoon's fear-stricken face was very satisfying to see, but it was not enough.

"If you value your life, you are going to tell me who helped you poison the King."

His eyes betrayed him before he could even deny it. "Don't bother trying to lie. I know you had a hand in it and probably your daughter, too."

"She did not, I swear. She would never have agreed to cause him harm," he claimed. Serenity tightened her hand on the dagger. "You're pathetic and I won't waste my time on you. In fact, if you tell me who you were working with, I won't let the King know that you were a part of it." Yoon looked doubtful.

"You doing this isn't surprising, but whoever came up with this plan- the one who set this in motion- he's the one I want. In return for that name, not only do you get your life, but I will also give you something else; something you desperately want." Yoon's eyes lifted, intrigued. "In a few weeks, I will leave and I won't come back. So, you don't have to worry about trying to get rid of me. You're even going to help me when that time comes." Yoon looked so confused, but also like he was seriously considering her offer. "For this to work, you must keep it to yourself. No one can know about this, not even your daughter. Do we have a deal?"

Yoon carefully considered her offer.

"Yes." The two stared at one another, their hatred for each other clear.

"Give me the name."

"You give me your word my daughter and I will not be implicated?"

"Yes."

"Kyril." The word made her heart drop. His smiling face and kind words every time she interacted with him flashed in her mind. All his support, all his advice, had been nothing but a ruse. She almost didn't want to expose him, not knowing how Kang-Dae would react. She wished she didn't know. As she thought more about it, she realized how deep this might go. What else had he done? What else had he had his hand in? All those times he was being helpful, how often was he just setting them up for his own malicious intents. She thought back to the attack on Amir and his men. Had that been him as well? Had he been the one responsible for the thefts, the contaminated food… all of it? All this time she'd been trying to convince herself Kang-Dae was the enemy, but the real enemy wore the mask of an ally.

CHAPTER FIFTY-ONE

Kang-Dae had been waiting on Serenity's return for a while. His anxiety was getting the best of him and he feared he would lose the nerve to go through with his decision to confess everything to her. He was about to search Serenity out just as she entered. A frown slowly came on his face as he took in her dark expression. "What is it?" She went to sit at the table asking him to join her. There was a feeling of dread that began to settle in his stomach.

When she started speaking about poisoning and conspiracy, his dread slowly turned to anger. The fact that someone would dare to try and manipulate him in such a vile way made him sick. His distorted memories and misplaced anger suddenly made sense. "I will find who is responsible," he swore to her.

"I already know," she said softly. He had not expected that. The sad look in her eyes was telling him he was not going to like what she had to say. She opened her mouth and closed it several times as if she were afraid to even speak. Finally, she took a breath and forced it out. "Kyril." Kang-Dae was sure that he had just heard her wrong. He was sure of it.

"Who?" He asked trying to focus so he could hear her correctly. She spoke as if it hurt her to repeat it. When she did, he realized he had heard her right. He shook his head. "No, you are mistaken." Kyril had been in his life since he was a child. He'd watched him at his father's side: always being there for him, serving him, advising him. It was why his father had made him a member, despite some hesitation from others. His father had trusted him up until his death and had always advised him to do the same.

"I'm so sorry, sweetie, but it's true."

"You're wrong," he said firmly. She just didn't realize the kind of person Kyril was. He was always someone Kang-Dae could count on. Every time the council tried to overrule him or put him down, it was always Kyril who stood behind him.

"Kang-Dae, I know you don't want to believe it-," He jumped up causing his chair to fall back with a loud clack. She visibly flinched. "How? How do you know this?" She was quiet. "Tell me!" He shouted moving forward. She scrambled away, genuine fear in her eyes. Kang-Dae stepped back.

"Why are you afraid of me?" He asked, completely baffled by her reaction. He would never hurt her, but she behaved like she was terrified- like he would attack her. Even now she stared at him with a fearful expression. He took a step toward her and she took a step back instinctively. He reached out to touch her, and his eyes moved toward the scratches on his arm. The scratches looked to be defensive marks, as if someone had done it to him. Her face was in his head staring at him with the same fearful expression. He was holding his hands on her throat as she tried to frantically get him to stop. The hurt and terrified look in her eyes as he squeezed the life from her was too much. His eyes teared up and he came back from what he knew was a memory from his missing days. Horrified over his actions he stumbled backward, away from her.

Serenity knew the moment he remembered what he'd done. The horror in his face the way he backed away from her as if he were afraid he'd do it again; it hurt her to see it. "It's alright," she tried to assure him, but he kept moving away.

"How could I-," he started staring at his hands.

"It wasn't you," she tried to tell him, but he didn't appear to hear her.

"I hurt you. I almos-," he started over his words unable to finish. Seeing him spinning out of control, Serenity quickly overcame her initial panic and took his face in her hands.

"I'm okay. We're fine. It wasn't your fault. It was all Kyril. He wanted you to kill me. He used the toxin to turn you against me. You weren't in control of yourself," she explained.

"Forgive me," he begged, his eyes desperate. "Please. I am so sorry." She wiped at his tears.

"There's nothing to forgive. I know you would never hurt me. I know that." He was still so disturbed by the memory of his deed he couldn't stop asking for forgiveness. "It's Kyril I want retribution from, not you," she told him. Remembering the cause of his terrible sin seemed to bring him back to his senses. What was once unimaginable guilt and sadness, changed to realization and outrage. She watched a rage build up in him. Kang-Dae pulled away from her and stormed out clearly on a mission. Not wanting him to be alone, she quickly followed after him.

CHAPTER FIFTY-TWO

Kang-Dae's mind was focused on one thing. He marched through the halls of the palace searching for his target. Serenity may have been behind, him but he did not notice. His target stood with his back to him speaking to Amir and Yu. The other two could see him coming and their eyes became wide as he appeared, giving Kyril only a two-second warning before Kang-Dae came up behind him. Forcing him to face him, he punched Kyril hard in the face. The other councilmen gasped. Amir tried to restrain him, but Jung-Soo was quick to pull the man back.

"Why?!" Kang-Dae roared. Kyril didn't answer, still trying to recover from the blow he received. "How could you do this to me? How?!" Kyril stared up at him unmoving. He appeared to be contemplating his next move.

"My King, I do-,"

"Do you want your last moments to be filled with more lies." realizing the severity of the situation, Kyril wiped his bleeding lip with the back of his hand and pulled himself up. To Kang-Dae, it was like witnessing a transformation. The once supportive and kind man he'd known his whole life, now appeared cold and unremorseful.

"How can you not know?" His change in tone and personality threw Kang-Dae. "My people are strong. We are meant to be leaders. Instead, we are forced to bow to you as if you are superior. Your great grandfather took control of us as if it was his right!" He raged. "When Katsuo invaded, I saw an opportunity to undo a great wrong. I waited years for this chance. Lowering myself so that you and your father would trust me, allowing me to lead you exactly where I wanted you."

Kang-Dae felt a stab in his heart from every word that fell from his mouth. "Lei Wei wasn't enough, but Katsuo will be. I wish I could be there to see him wipe you all out." Kang-Dae balked at the realization that it was Kyril who was responsible for losing so many to the warlord. "Unfortunately, I failed at disposing of your seer. It seemed no matter what I tried she survived."

"You were working with Amin," Kang-Dae realized. Kyril shrugged. He turned those malevolent eyes to Serenity. Kang-Dae wanted to gouge them out for even attempting to look at her.

"I am sorry, my dear. I have nothing against you personally. I just couldn't have you discovering the truth. Also, I knew taking you from him would hurt him more than any wound I could inflict."

"You will die for this," Kang-Dae swore.

"I die proudly knowing I did everything I could to bring down the Xianian hold over my land."

Kang-Dae stepped closer to him. "You truly have no remorse?" he asked, a small part of him hoping to see a glimpse of the man he'd always known.

"My only regret is that I won't be around to watch this city fall; and personally see you and all these greedy fools put down like the dogs you are," Kang-Dae charged at his once most trusted advisor. He could think of nothing except making him pay for every evil deed with his bare hands. He was so consumed with his anger, he didn't see Kyril pull out the dagger. He barely had time to catch Kyril's hands, stopping the tip a mere few inches from his stomach. He struggled with him. The older man was strong, perhaps even stronger than him. Kang-Dae's arms shook as he tried to keep the dagger from penetrating him, but he was slowly losing his hold. He couldn't keep this up much longer. Taking a chance, he started pushing Kyril's arms to the side. Just as Kang-Dae's hold weakened, Kyril plowed forward-only managing to slash Kang-Dae's side. Kang-Dae didn't dwell on the pain of the sharp blade hitting his skin. He took advantage of Kyril's loss of balance to turn and slam his elbow into Kyril's stomach. Grunting Kyril stumbled back. Kang-Dae spun around and kicked him right in the chest. The older man went flying, landing in a heap on the floor, the dagger falling from his hands. Kang-Dae stalked toward him, scooping up the dagger. Kyril was coughing, spitting out small amounts of blood. He stared up at Kang-Dae, defiantly raising his head.

"I curse you and this forsaken country. My spirit will haunt these walls for all eternity. You will never know peace, nor happiness again." Kang-Dae slammed the dagger down, and as he did, he could hear Serenity's shocked gasp from behind him.

Kyril opened his eyes. He turned to look at the dagger embed in the floor an inch from him. "Lock him away. Tomorrow have him taken back to his true home." Kyril looked at him, confusion in his eyes. "Then tear him limb from limb, so he can be buried all over the country he loved so much."

A speck of fear entered Kyril's gaze, but he soon began to chuckle, then laugh. The guards grabbed him and hauled him away. His maniacal laughter echoing behind them.

CHAPTER FIFTY-THREE

Witnessing Kyril's confession and hearing Kang-Dae sentence him to death was hard for Serenity. Not because the man hadn't earned his death, but because she had known how much it pained Kang-Dae. Kang-Dae had been so heartbroken by Kyril's betrayal. She tried to be there for him as best as she could, but there was so little she could do to comfort him. His whole world had been shaken, and she couldn't fix it for him. She took comfort in the fact that Kyril would no longer be around to manipulate anyone else. She could be a little more at ease with leaving, knowing he was no longer lurking around. She only had Yoon to worry about, but she already had plans for him. For now, she could use him.

Serenity ticked off another day on her makeshift calendar. 20 days until the next blessed moon. She needed to get to work on her exit strategy. For that, she'd need more allies.

Amoli had come by to bring her a new dress. "I need your help," Serenity said.

"Of course, my Queen."

"You can't repeat this to anyone- not even the King, do you understand?" Uncertainty came upon her face, but she nodded nonetheless, proving to Serenity that her trust in her loyalty was not misplaced.

"I'm going home." Confusion spread on her pretty face.

"But I thought you could not."

"It wasn't the right day," she explained.

"Will the King-."

"He can't know."

"Why?" Amoli asked, becoming even more baffled.

"Because he would try to stop me," Serenity told her.

Amoli shook her head. "He would help as he did before," she said confidently.

"He knew about it, Amoli. He knew it was the wrong day." Amoli grew quiet. She started to shake her head in denial. "It's true. He never wanted me to leave, so he tried to make me think I couldn't."

"He must have had a reason," she said asserted.

"I know he has feelings for me, and those feelings made him try to protect me. But it's not right." Amoli looked like she wanted to argue but clearly could come up with no explanations as to why he had done what he did.

"Will you help me?" She asked once more. Now that Amoli knew what was at stake, she hesitated. Serenity knew it was a hard thing she was asking, but she needed her friend. Amoli looked her in the eyes.

"Yes, my Queen."

Serenity pulled the woman into a hug, grateful to have her.

***

Satori sat alone in his room reflecting. He had been doing a lot of reflecting lately, especially since Kyril's death. Knowing of his many betrayals, and how easily he and many others had been manipulated by Kyril, disturbed him. Satori never would have thought he'd be a traitor. He'd always looked down on the man because of his origins, but he never truly questioned his loyalty to the King. For the first time, Satori began to wonder about the virtue of the council. He always thought they were needed to help keep the King on the right path, but perhaps the opposite was true. First, Amin, now Kyril. Were they all just greedy and spiteful men out for themselves, believing they were right and better? He thought he did what he had done for his people, but now he wasn't so sure. Kyril was able to foresee Satori's abandonment of Amir that day, almost leading to the young man's death and many of their soldiers. His pride and self-righteousness had been used against him and his country. Satori was rethinking a lot of things now. What he saw as trouble now seemed necessary. Maybe he had been wrong about the Queen and her role in their kingdom. If not for her, who knows what would have become of them. He wondered over his own actions and feelings. Was he just like them? Did he deserve to be a man with power? How had he used it? Was he as honorable as he thought? Had eight years on the council warped his senses and made him forget what his true duty was? It hurt to think about. How long before he crossed the line like the others and brought disgrace to his family and his name? Had he already done so?

***

Jae-Hwa lay on her bed, locked away in her room. She'd denied entry to all servants and her father as well. The news about Kyril had put her in a state of shock. She had been so desperate to be queen, she'd allowed herself to be used by such a man- a traitor. His goal had never been about protecting the country from an unworthy ruler, it had been to cause the King's downfall. And she had helped him. The nauseous feeling in her stomach intensified. She watched as the man she thought she would love forever was tormented by their manipulations, thinking it was fine as long as it got her the crown. How could she ever have thought she was worthy of being queen? She had almost helped in the destruction of her country because she yearned for a title that had never been hers in the first place. Jae-Hwa had hoped this would cause a realization in her father. She had pleaded with him to join her in returning home. This palace brought out the worst in them both. If they had any chance of repentance and living decent lives, they could not stay. He'd dismissed her, telling her that despite Kyril's evil intention, he had paved a way for them. She didn't know what he was speaking of, so she gave up. Regardless of what he did, she would be leaving this life behind.

CHAPTER FIFTY-FOUR

Amoli stood next to Arezoo, watching nervously as her Queen stared down Councilman Yoon. She'd been more than surprised when her Queen admitted the man would be a part of her plan. The man's hatred of her was well known, but maybe that was why she decided to use him. No one would want her gone more than him.

"What exactly do you need from me?" Yoon scowled.

"I want you to push your daughter's trip home back a couple of days," Serenity told him.

"Why?"

"Because I'm going to accompany her as Queen to see her off and visit a part of the kingdom I've never seen before. On the way, we'll make a detour."

"The King would never let you go alone," Yoon pointed out.

"I will handle him. You just make the arrangements."

"I will not leave my daughter alone with you," he spoke indignantly. "I will go as well,"

"Whatever you like," she said sarcastically.

"If this is some kind of trick-," he warned.

"Do you want me gone or not? I told you, once this is over, I'll be out of your way forever."

"You would truly give up your position, your throne?" he asked in disbelief.

"Don't worry about my reasons, just do your part," she told him. Yoon narrowed his eyes at her before he nodded stiffly. He turned and left.

"Is it wise to trust him with this?" Arezoo questioned and Amoli agreed.

"For once, Yoon actually has a use." To say that Serenity had been more than a little shocked when she heard Jae-Hwa was leaving the palace was an understatement. She hadn't seen the woman in days. She was sure hell would have had to freeze over for her to give up her notions of being queen. But Serenity saw an opportunity. The path to Yenoa would take them right past the lake. Now that she had a genuine excuse to leave, they could enact their plan without fear of suspicion. It was why she hadn't turned Yoon in.

"He helped poison our King. He tried to get him to kill you. Will you allow him to get away with that?"

"I swore that if he gave up Kyril I wouldn't implicate him in that." Serenity tugged lightly on her necklace. Arezoo and Amoli did not look pleased with that.

"Besides, once I'm gone, Arezoo's going to arrest him."

Both women looked up at her with matching expressions of bewilderment.

"You swore you would not expose him," Amoli repeated her words back to her.

"For the poisoning," Serenity clarified. "Arezoo's going to arrest him for my murder."

Arezoo's eye twitched and Amoli gawked at her.

"Murder, my Queen?"

"When I'm gone, the people will want to know what happened to the Queen. Yoon, someone who is well known for hating me, will just so happen to be there when I disappear forever without a trace, after he so kindly asked me to accompany him and his daughter. The people would condemn him based on that alone," Serenity explained to the women, shocking them both. "There's no way in hell I'm going to let him get away with what he did to my husband," she continued, her face hardening.

Arezoo was impressed, the corner of her mouth turning upward slightly. Amoli, however, looked unsure.

"We don't have much time left. Arezoo, I need you to keep an eye on Yoon. Make sure he doesn't try to make any special arrangements of his own." Arezoo agreed. With a bow, she took her leave.

"My Queen, are you sure about this?" asked Amoli. Things had gotten so much better between her and the King. She would hate to see how her leaving would affect him.

Before Serenity could answer, Nasreen announced "Advisor Min!" from the other side of the door. The ladies only had a two-second notice before he came in. His eyes went from both of them to the map still laid out on the table.

"Did you want something?" Serenity asked. Min sighed heavily.

"You have been busy." Serenity said nothing, just waited for him to get to the point. "I spoke with the King's scholars. I know you've been asking about the next blessed moon."

"I was curious," Serenity deflected.

"You are trying to return home."

Serenity crossed her arms. "Why do you care?" she demanded. "You wanted me gone as soon as I got here. You should be glad to see me go."

Min shook his head. "I'd hoped you'd prove me wrong about you," he uttered, shaking his head in disappointment that only angered Serenity. What right did he have to judge her? He must have known about Kang-Dae's deception as well.

"Excuse me?"

"I feared you would bring strife to our King and the land. There were moments I thought I was mistaken. At times you've proven yourself to be very competent as Queen." The compliment surprised her. "But your effect on my King still worried me. His attachment to you was dangerous. When he made you his wife my biggest concern was always for him. I was able to overlook many things when I thought you cared for him. But now, I see that my initial assumption was correct."

Serenity slammed her hand down on the desk, offended and angered at the man's audacity. "You have no idea what I feel or felt. You have no idea what he tried to take from me."

"He saved you."

"He trapped me!"

"You would have died." The news took her voice and her anger; she felt Amoli stiffen at her side. "That was what he kept from you. All those who arrived on the night of the blessed moon, they like you appeared out of nowhere. But unlike you, they were all dead. That was why they considered you a witch. You were the first to survive, and that may have only been because Hui was there to revive you. Do you think you'll be so lucky again?" Serenity stood in stunned silence.

"That- that can't be true."

"Do you think I would make it up? As you said, it would have been a relief to see you gone back then. I am ashamed to admit, a part of me wanted to keep the truth from him- to let him believe otherwise. But I didn't want your blood on my hands."

Serenity looked away unable to handle his penetrating stare, screaming the truth of his words.

After dropping his bombshell, Min left. Serenity clutched at her necklace. It was all too much to handle. Amoli tried to speak to her, but she couldn't hear anything she said. Once again, fate threw a curveball at her and this time she didn't think she could avoid it.

CHAPTER FIFTY-FIVE

Serenity sat in her study staring into space. She'd sent Amoli away unable to look at the pitying look on her face any longer. She felt like crying, but she honestly didn't think she had any more tears to shed. What was she supposed to do now? Back at square one with even less hope than before. Could she die trying to get home? Suddenly, her dream was starting to make sense. The shadow must have been death. If she had succeeded in returning, she would not have made it back alive, which is why she never made it in the dream. Kang-Dae had known all along. He truly had been trying to protect her from herself.

When Kang-Dae first brought up the possibility of things going wrong on her trip, she dismissed it. She just assumed she made it here fine, so she could make it back fine. But, now she recalled the terrible coldness that had seeped inside her and the fact that she'd been unconscious for several days afterward. When she did wake up, she felt drained- like the life had been sucked out of her; and maybe it had. But she survived right? Couldn't she do it again? Even as she questioned herself, she felt her chances were nonexistent.

Was this what Kang-Dae had struggled with when he found out? Had he gone back and forward on whether to tell her and destroy her hope of returning home? Would she have even believed him? Just thinking about it made her heart lurch with guilt. How horrible she'd been to him, how callous. She thought the worst of him when in actuality he had been doing what he'd done since she'd arrived: protecting her. She recalled the guilt in his eyes and his apology that night under the stars. He looked so tormented. It had hurt him to lie to her. Even when she suffered due to his lie, he had suffered along with her. That night she thought she would go home, he looked so ashamed. She imagined it must have been so difficult for him. A man of such honor having to deceive someone they cared about in such a way. It explained the distant look in his eyes that was always present. Even when they'd been on good terms, and every moment for her felt precious and memorable, he always looked as though he wasn't worthy of it or her. He faced it all alone for her and the idea of it tore her heart.

***

Kang-Dae sat on his throne speaking to what was left of his counsel. With the death of Kyril, he felt things needed to be talked through. He needed to be more diligent about who he kept around. He needed to know who was actually here for the kingdom and who was here for themselves. There had been too much betrayal, selfishness, and unknown grudges. This couldn't happen again. The doors burst open and his Queen came in. He sat up straighter as she walked in with purpose.

"Leave!" she shot it with such a commanding voice his counsel only hesitated for a moment before filing out one by one. After they were alone, she climbed up the steps towards him. She looked distraught and he became fearful that something awful might have happened. She stopped in front of him, her eyes brimming with unshed tears.

He wanted to ask what was wrong, but before he could even say a word she was climbing into his lap kissing him almost desperately. He was stunned, unable to react fast enough. He could taste the tears on her lips as she practically devoured him. It was like she was trying to climb into him. He broke free and grabbed her face in his hands. Her eyes were wild yet pleading. She was out of breath, but she was still determined for more. She leaned in again, this time going for his throat. Kang-Dae bit back a moan. A million questions circled in his mind, but all he could focus on was her soft lips. Feeling her shift on top of him, his eyes widened at the sight of her attempt to remove her overlay.

Pulling back, he stopped her. She released a frustrated whimper. "Serenity," he said softly, raising her eyes to his. Her chin quivered and she released a sob. Kang-Dae took her in his arms as she cried.

Serenity slowly came to her senses. She knew she probably should get up, but her legs had fallen asleep. In light of her actions, she now felt embarrassed over her wanton behavior. It was hard to even meet his eyes because she wanted to hide. She felt the need to explain herself just a little. "I," She began not sure how to explain what had gotten into her. He cut her off with a soft kiss. He stared at her with loving and gentle eyes. She intended to finally put everything in the open, to talk about what he'd done and what she learned. But when she saw him, she became so overcome with everything she could not find the words. Her body acted on its own accord.

He helped her stand and awkwardly resituated her clothes, not speaking or attempting to make sense of what had just happened.

***

Serenity's eyes stared at the walls in the dark room. Sleep alluded her that night. She was too filled with heavy thoughts. She clung to Kang-Dae's arm around her. Serenity started to imagine a life with him, something she'd been too afraid to do before. With the chances of her returning home seemingly dashed once again, she felt she had to open herself up to the possibility. If she allowed herself to truly give up, what would she be gaining? She could almost see it: sitting by his side running the kingdom together, supporting one another; doing work in the city- maybe even teaching again. She imagined mornings with him: awakening in his arms each day, the gift of a gentle kiss every time she opened her eyes. She thought of playing games with Amoli and her long talks with Jung-Soo. She even dared to imagine a child. She could almost see her running through the halls with laughter as Kang-Dae chased her. A beautiful child with her curls and her father's eyes. The vision became too much, and she stopped. It all sounded nice- blissful even, but she couldn't forget that it came with a heavy price; the price of her family's peace of mind. The price of never seeing them again. If she truly gave in now, she was giving up on them. Would she be giving in to fear if she didn't even try to return? God had protected her the first time. Was she choosing to believe he wouldn't do it again? Or was she being too optimistic? Was this where she was meant to be? Or maybe this was a test of her conviction and faith.

How could she live happily knowing home was at her fingertips, but she had been too scared to try? Didn't she owe it to her family to do anything and everything possible to make it back to them? Wouldn't it be selfish to move on? Those thoughts played through her mind all night. She needed guidance, someone to talk to. But she knew those she would want to go to would only tell her to stay. They'd encourage that part of herself that wanted the life she'd envisioned. They didn't understand what she would be giving up, the heartache she could cause. No, there was no happiness to be had here if she didn't try. Making her decision, she felt no relief or excitement. Instead, that overwhelming grief she'd had the night she'd thought her family was lost to her forever, had returned only now it was for her new family.

CHAPTER FIFTY-SIX

When Serenity revealed to Amoli she still intended

to go home, the woman couldn't believe it. "You still mean

to go through with it?" Serenity nodded.

"I have to."

"No, you don't. My Queen, what can you achieve

by throwing away your life so carelessly?" Serenity had

never heard Amoli's voice so strong.

"I'm not."

"You heard what Min said," Amoli brought up.

Serenity let out a sigh.

"I heard what a bunch of superstitious men told

him."

"It was those same superstitious men who told you

about the moon, and you believed that." Serenity didn't

have a response to that. "Maybe you need to consider-," Amoli began.

"No."

"My Queen," pleaded Amoli.

"I'm going home. It's going to work this time."

"Did you have a vision?" Amoli asked. Serenity's eyes shifted as that dream resurfaced once more, the memory of that shadow making her shudder.

"It doesn't matter."

"What did you see?" Amoli demanded.

"It's going to work this time," repeated Serenity.

"If your dreams are trying to warn you from making a mistake, you have to heed them."

"I didn't dream anything," she lied, but Amoli wasn't buying it.

"I know you want to be with your family. I know how important it is for you to have them know you are safe. But if given the choice to have you here and alive or with them and dead, you know what they would choose." Serenity did not want to hear Amoli voicing the very things she spent all night suppressing. Of course, all of Amoli's concerns were valid. But if she let them back in, the fear would return along with the doubts and she couldn't afford that. She couldn't falter on this.

She placed her hands on Amoli's shoulders. "I know it's hard for you to understand this. But I need you to trust me. This is going to work. I know it." Amoli searched her eyes, trying to find anything that suggested she would not go through with it. Finding nothing, Amoli pulled away from Serenity.

"I will not help lead you to your death!" she shouted, storming out of the room.

That anxiousness returned. Serenity hated to see Amoli so angry with her, but there was nothing she could say to comfort her. This was something she had to do.

CHAPTER FIFTY–SEVEN

Kang-Dae was alone in their bed. The sun was up, but it didn't feel too late. He knew he'd fallen asleep wrapped around Serenity. He sat up to find her just as she came strolling into the room with a tray in her hands. A servant was behind her with another. They set the trays down and Serenity thanked her for her help. When she noticed he was awake, the smile she directed towards him made his heart skip. She sent the servant on her way before rushing back to bed- practically jumping in, making him laugh. She kissed him softly. "Good morning," she said in Xianian. He returned the kiss and the greeting.

"Why are you up so early?" he asked.

"I wanted to get things ready."

"Ready for what?"

"We're playing hooky today."

"Hoo-key?" She quickly explained the tradition in her land where young people would avoid studies and responsibilities for a day without their parents' knowledge. It sounded like something he would have loved to participate in when he was young. "Why today?"

"Because I think you deserve a break and we should take some time for us," she said with conviction. Kang-Dae thought about it. He knew there were many things they could be doing, but like always he couldn't deny her.

Their day started with breakfast, which she gingerly fed him in bed. She doted on him and fed him from chopsticks and her fingers- which he couldn't help nipping at lovingly, making her laugh. Once breakfast was done, she read to him as he lay on her lap holding her hand to his chest. Her reading had become much better. There was less hesitation now, and her pronunciations were like a native Xianian. Later they went riding, enjoying a leisurely trot around the palace walls. They even had a race that he easily won, to her annoyance. He had teased her, laughing at her pout but he kissed it away. They enjoyed lunch in the garden with his mother. He enjoyed seeing the two interacting, talking like mother and daughter. Although, he could have done without the moments when they both turned on him, brought up supposedly bad habits he had and talked amongst themselves about him like he wasn't there.

Following that, they played a game in their chambers which she won, and spent several minutes mercilessly teasing him for his loss and his surprising lack of skills. They ate dinner on the balcony under the stars in a comfortable silence, giving one another soft and loving smiles the entire time. He realized at that moment everything he'd eaten that day had been his favorite foods. She must have purposely requested and picked every meal. He felt grateful, grateful for her. Her bright smile and happy behavior made him feel happy. They lay together under the stars. To his surprise, she began to sing. Her voice was so soft and soothing. He of course, didn't recognize the song, but it didn't matter. The day had been so perfect it was like a dream. He couldn't help thinking this would be their future. He even conjured up an image of her heavy with his child one day. He wanted that with her, but he knew he couldn't have it unless he told her the truth. After the Kyril incident, he'd put it off, unable to deal with her possible hatred of him on top of losing Kyril. Now, he knew had to come clean and pray she would not hate him.

"Serenity," he called out. She turned to him. He swallowed, trying to work up the courage to speak. "There's something you need to know." If he looked at her, he didn't think he could get through it. So, he kept his eyes on her necklace, focusing on the small purple flower inside. "That night when you tried to return home, I-,"

"I know." She said effectively stunning him into silence. "Min told me."

Kang-Dae didn't know what to feel. His heart was pounding in his ears. "But-, ho-, why," he stammered, unable to form words. She placed her finger on his lips and she kissed them.

For a moment, he thought maybe she didn't really know what he'd done- or maybe it hadn't truly dawned on her yet. "I'm sor-," he started only for her to kiss him again, longer. Kang-Dae was truly baffled. Of all the reactions he'd imagined, this was not one of them. She stared at him with warmth in her eyes, instead of the resentment he'd prepared for. She kissed him once more, this time he returned it. The burden and guilt he'd been carrying for months was being washed away with every brush of her lips. All his fears and worries dissolved as he pulled her closer to him so he could hold her. When she pulled away, he had a moment of fear that she'd suddenly come to her senses. She stood up and reached her hand out to him. Relieved, he accepted it, pulling himself up and letting her lead him inside.

Serenity walked them over to the bed and sat him on the edge. Kang-Dae tilted his head quizzically, unsure of what she was doing until her hands went to the sash on her dress. Mouth dry, he could do nothing but swallow as the dress dropped to the floor. Serenity stood before him in nothing but her undergarments; Kang-Dae's heart raced. Serenity stepped between his legs, wrapping her arms around his neck. She kissed him slowly, taking her time. Kang-Dae slid his arms around her waist. His hands went to the tie on her top. With a tug, the thread loosened. Never breaking their kiss, Kang-Dae tightened his hold on her and rolled them both onto the bed. Serenity's hands were busy undoing his robe. Once it was open, he quickly shed it and tossed it. Feeling her hands roaming his bare skin, Kang-Dae shuddered. Like the night under stars, he kissed her fervently. The rest of their clothes were quickly discarded. His eyes locked with hers, one question within them. Serenity nodded and brought him down to kiss her again.

He made love to her slowly, savoring every moment. But he planned on even more moments in the future. She held his face in her palm not taking her eyes off him as they moved together in an intimate dance. He gently kissed the inside of her hand not stopping his movements. She was so beautiful to him and she finally felt like she was his. They pushed each other higher and higher, neither ready to tumble over the edge just yet- needing the moment to last as long as possible. Serenity cried out first, unable to contain it. She clutched at his back as his pace increased, reaching his peak with a loud groan.

He held her to him when it was over, never wanting to let her go. He kissed the top of her head as she snuggled into his embrace. "Saranghae," he whispered as he fell asleep blissfully, with a head full of dreams of Serenity.

CHAPTER FIFTY-EIGHT

Serenity had a tough time turning herself without waking Kang-Dae, but she did. She wanted to see his face. He looked so relaxed and peaceful. She lay there, trying to memorize every detail of it. She wanted it ingrained in her memory for all time. She lightly traced her fingers over his features. She wouldn't sleep tonight. She was taking as much time as she could with him. It was why she wanted today to be all about them. If it was to be their last day together, she wanted to give them both happy memories to hold onto. It had been both wonderful and agonizingly sad spending such precious moments together, knowing it was the end. Whether she survived her trip or not, she would not see him again.

The time had come. As the sun began to rise, her heartbeat did the same. She wished she had more time. She swallowed hard, preparing herself for what she was about to do. She quietly asked God to forgive her and closed her eyes. She started with a moan, then a groan. She moved a little, just enough to cause the bed to shift. She mimicked the movements of a person having a bad dream. It didn't take long for Kang-Dae to awaken. Immediately, he tried to "wake" her from her nightmare. He gently shook her, calling out her name. She opened her eyes slowly acting as if she had been in a deep sleep. Seeing the worried look on his face just made the guilt that much worse.

"Are you alright?" He asked, helping her sit up. She took her time acting as if she needed a moment to recover.

"I saw- I saw a red bird getting caught in a trap. It couldn't get out. Then a tiger tore it from the net." Kang-Dae's brows furrowed.

"The western plains are overrun with robins. The people there are hunters. It is where most of our meat comes from. We have not gotten word that Katsuo had entered their lands yet- perhaps that's their next stop," he wondered out loud.

"Maybe the tiger represents our soldiers stopping them," she offered with false sincerity.

"Do you think this will happen soon?"

"I think so. We can't afford to wait."

He nodded and began to get up. "The trip to the Gi lands?"

"I'll take care of it. It will be fine."

He kissed her and hopped out of bed. Her heart burned over her lies and deceit. Is this how he had felt when he had done the same to her?

***

She and Amoli saw him and Jung-Soo off. "Safe travels, my King," Amoli said handing him a pack. He looked strangely at it before offering her his thanks. Serenity held back her tears as she said goodbye to Jung-Soo, hoping not to alert him. She had to resist the urge to hug him. He looked at her a bit strangely, but his mind must have been preoccupied with the upcoming battle because he didn't say anything. Before Kang-Dae could get to his horse Serenity wrapped her arms around his neck and kissed him hard; her last goodbye. The smile he had when they pulled away almost destroyed her, but she held her composure. "I will be back," he promised.

"I know," she said. Reaching for her necklace, she removed it and placed it over his head. He looked at it then at her, questioning her with his eyes. "For luck," was all she said. He kissed her once more, appearing a lot happier than a man going into battle probably should be. As he rode off on his fruitless endeavor, Serenity felt her heart breaking. She couldn't stop the tears from falling.

"My Queen?" Amoli asked. Serenity waved her off, unable to speak. There was no going back now.

Serenity, Arezoo, Yoon, Jae-Hwa, and their accompanied men traveled by horse and carriage. She and Jae-Hwa rode in the carriage. She'd forced Yoon to ride on a horse, not wanting to be confined in such a small space with him. They traveled in silence with nothing but her fears and doubts speaking loudly in her mind. She kept rebuking the idea she was heading toward her death. She prayed continuously that she would make it through safely. Her eyes drifted to Jae-Hwa who was almost unrecognizable. She wore simple clothes and had swept up her long hair into a ponytail. Her entire aura was different. Serenity couldn't fathom what brought about this change in her. The hoofbeats of the horses were the only sounds breaking through the carriage walls. The women never spoke or acknowledged one another, both too caught up in their introspections to attempt a conversation. Serenity thought about Amoli, wishing she was there with her. But she'd been adamant about not being involved in what she believed was a suicidal endeavor. She hadn't even told her goodbye, which had stung. Serenity could only hope she could forgive her one day.

***

Amoli raced to up the temple steps. She'd sprinted the whole way through the grounds in search of the Queen Dowager. The older woman was just leaving the temple with her guards following close behind her when Amoli came upon her. "Your Majesty," Amoli addressed out of breath.

"What is it?" asked concern all over her face.

"You have to stop her," Amoli gasped out.

"Stop who?"

"The Queen. She's trying to return home, but it will kill her." the Dowager Queen paled and clutched her chest. She looked to her guard.

"Gather my men and bring them to me!"

CHAPTER FIFTY-NINE

Kang-Dae had Serenity on the brain as he rode. The night came up quickly, so he made his garrison set up camp. He sat by the fire, staring into it. He hoped for a short quick victory so he could return to his wife. He would resume his vow of making her as happy as possible. Only now, there would be no secrets lurking between them stealing the joy he felt. Memories of their passionate night together were on repeat in his mind. It filled him with indescribable joy to think that they would have hundreds of more nights like that. One day, they might be blessed with a child. The idea only recently entered his mind, now he couldn't stop wanting it. And he knew Serenity would want it too. She had a motherly heart. He could imagine her teaching and molding their child, nurturing and raising them to be just as amazing as she was.

The men passed around bread. Kang-Dae ate distractedly. Jung-Soo was quiet as usual, but he did appear to have something on his mind. Kang-Dae played with Serenity's necklace, smiling to at the memory of her giving it to him. He suddenly remembered the pack Amoli had given to him. He had been confused as to why she had personally packed it for him. She had never made such a gesture before. It wasn't her responsibility and he already had plenty of provisions, but he took it anyway so he wouldn't upset her. She clearly spent time on it. When he opened the pack, the first thing he saw were various fruits. Just as he was about to offer them to his comrades, he noticed the small paper sticking to the side. He picked it up, reading the writing on it. As he turned it over, his heart dropped seeing the words that were written.

'She's going home.'

The pack fell to the ground as he stood, fruit going everywhere. "We're leaving!" he shouted. His men looked at him as if he were crazy. Jung-Soo was also staring at him confused. Kang-Dae slammed the paper in his chest. He watched as Jung-Soo's eyes widen as he read it.

"We have to go, now," he declared. Now understanding his panic, Jung-Soo ordered the men to pack up quickly.

"Now!" Kang-Dae roared.

This got them moving. Everyone gathered their things. Kang-Dae was the first on his horse. He didn't even care if he left his men behind. The only thing on his mind was getting to Serenity.

***

They stopped for the night at the insistence of Jae-Hwa. Serenity didn't want to waste any more time, but she gave in. Kang-Dae was at least two days in the opposite direction, so she had time before he would even begin to realize what she had done. They set up camp not far from the road. It was odd seeing someone as dainty as Jae-Hwa sitting on the ground, even with the various blankets she had under her. Serenity wasn't in the mood to sleep, so she sat up staring at the fire. Arezoo stood close by keeping watch.

"What is the real reason you wished to join me on my journey home?" Jae-Hwa asked.

"Why did you decide to go home in the first place?" Serenity countered. Jae-Hwa was quiet at first, the light of the fire dancing across her face.

"I finally realized the truth," she finally spoke.

"What truth?"

"From the time that I could talk, I was told who I was, what I wanted, and who I was going to be. All my thoughts, wishes, dreams- they had never been my own. The King helped me realize, in his own way, that I do not know who I am."

This was not something Serenity had expected would ever come out of Jae-Hwa's mouth. "The person who I was trying to be, was only causing myself and others pain. I no longer wish to live my life that way. I am going home because I am hoping I can discover myself. As much as I do not know who I am, I know for certain I will not find her in the palace."

Serenity gave her a thoughtful look. She sounded genuine. Serenity applauded her growth, knowing very few people ever reevaluated themselves and made the decision to change. "I hope you find her." Jae-Hwa smiled.

"Me too."

The sounds of the forest comforted them. "You are very fortunate," Serenity raised her brow.

"Because I'm queen?" Jae-Hwa shook her head.

"The King's love for you is obvious." Serenity suddenly became interested in the fire in front of her. "With so much against you- Satori, Kyril, my father, me," she added remorsefully. "His love for you would not dim. Not everyone will experience such devotion." The pain in her heart grew listening to her words. The irony of the woman who repeatedly tried to steal her husband from her unwittingly making her feel even more guilty for leaving him, was not lost on Serenity. Serenity excused herself before she fell apart in front of her.

She leaned against the tree letting the tears flow freely. Arezoo came up behind her, a handkerchief in hand. She accepted it with a soft thank you. Arezoo tapped her on the shoulder to get her to look at her. Without words, she conveyed exactly what she wanted to ask her. Reading her perfectly, she shook her head. "I'm going home," she said firmly. Arezoo looked a bit unsure, but in the end she nodded and walked back to camp, helping her onto her pallet. Tomorrow, one way or another, she would disappear; leaving everything behind.

CHAPTER SIXTY

Serenity and company arrived at the lake by nightfall. The moon was just as big and bright as it was on that meaningful night beneath the stars with Kang-Dae. She swallowed the lump in her throat that came about just thinking of him. As planned, Yoon was at the carriage telling Jae-Hwa to continue, claiming they'd catch up. She and her men left. The rest of them: Serenity, Arezoo, Yoon, and one of his men, stayed behind.

As they got closer to their destination, Arezoo made everyone stop. She must have seen something in the distance because she motioned for them to be quiet and moved off to the road. They quietly went into the trees and dismounted.

"What is it?" Serenity asked.

"They are waiting for us." Eyes wide, Serenity turned her gaze forward, she squinted in an attempt to see through the darkness. She didn't see anything. But as she listened closely, there was the unmistakable sounds of shuffling feet and murmuring voices.

"What are they doing here?" Yoon asked his face tight. Serenity and Arezoo shared a look. 'Amoli.' They both knew it at the same time. She'd been so distant and shady before they left. "What do we do?" Yoon asked desperately, not wanting to see this opportunity turning to dust in front of him. Serenity thought about her choices. They had no way of knowing how many of them there were, so fighting through was not a viable option. She thought hard trying to recall the layout of the lake. There was a ridge overlooking the lake that was directly above it. It may be her only chance.

"We'll go around and climb up." Realizing what she had planned, Arezoo stopped her with a hand.

"You can't know you can jump from that height and survive."

"I will. It's going to work. I won't even touch the bottom." Arezoo looked apprehensive, but Serenity didn't give her time to object and went in search of a way up.

Kang-Dae raced his horse down the road, refusing to allow it to slow even for a second. His men struggled to keep up behind him. He moved like a desperate man, fearing he was already too late. In the back of his mind, he wondered how long she'd been planning this. Memories of their last day together surfaced. She had been saying goodbye and he didn't even realize it. He pushed his horse harder.

Arriving at the lake, he was surprised to see his mother's men stationed there. She must have been warned just like he was. He approached one of them. "Has there been a sighting?"

"No, my King," the soldier answered.

"Keep an eye out. They cannot get through!"

"Yes, my King."

Kang-Dae searched around on his own, not trusting anyone else's eyes. He couldn't rely on these men. Serenity was determined. She wouldn't let them deter her. If she planned all of this, she was not about to just give up. His eyes went to the sky. The moon shone bright, giving off significant light. As his eyes lowered, his gaze fell upon the ridge. "Is anyone up there?" He asked pointing up.

"No, my King."

Kang-Dae took off for it, Jung-Soo following closely behind him.

CHAPTER SIXTY-ONE

Serenity took Arezoo's hand as she helped her up the rocky ridge. The climb hadn't been easy, especially in the dark. Her foot slipped more than once, but thankfully Arezoo had been there each time. She had no idea how Yoon was coping with the climb, but she didn't care. She didn't know why he insisted on accompanying them this far.

Serenity's heart was pounding once they made it to the top. She peeked over and felt a wave of dizziness hit her. Jumping made the ordeal 100 times scarier. She stood there, staring off the ridge. Now that she was here and there was nothing in her path, her trepidation was at an all-time high. This was the moment of truth. She was either about to go home or to her death. She took a closer look, careful not to be seen by the men at the bottom.

"Serenity!" Kang-Dae's voice rang out. Serenity's heart jumped and she spun around. Arezoo had already taken in a protective stance in front of her. Yoon moved off to the side, but his man moved closer to Serenity. Kang-Dae approached panic all over his face. As he came forward, Arezoo and Serenity took a step closer to the edge.

"Stop," she threatened. He froze.

"Wait!" he said. "We can talk about this."

"I'm sorry, but I have to go," she told him, taking another step back.

Kang-Dae shook his head. "Please, just wait a bit longer. I will find a way for you to get back safely. I swear it. Give me some time. I will search the whole world if I have to."

"Kang-Dae, you have to let me go. This is my decision." He came forward once more, but Arezoo stepped up blocking his path.

"Please, please Serenity. Do not do this. I know- I know I should have told you the truth sooner. Maybe then we could have come up with a way together, but I was so afraid of this moment. I do not want to lose you. I cannot lose you, not this way. Please, please, just stay," he begged. Serenity fought back tears as she slowly shook her head.

"I can't."

"You can; yes, you can. We can find a way, the both of us. Until then, you can be happy. We can be happy, I promise." Serenity's lip trembled and her shoulders shook.

"Maybe, maybe this is where you were meant to be," he tried to offer, desperately saying anything to get her to stay. Serenity swallowed hard and took one more step back. Kang-Dae fell to his knees, tears falling down his cheeks. "Do not leave. Please! I will do anything. You are my wife, my Queen! I need you- this country needs you. I can't lose you. Saranghae, saranghae!" He shouted out. Serenity froze, her heart pounded so hard it hurt. His words are penetrating her soul.

"I- I love you, too." she said with a sob. Hearing her confession, Kang-Dae stood. He reached for her. "Stay. Stay with me. Saranghae," He said once more. Serenity looked back toward the ridge and then to Kang-Dae, her husband- her love; something she tried to repress, but had been unable to. She'd loved him for a while now, regardless of how she tried to harden her heart to him. She may not have said it the way he did, but the feelings were there. She wanted to laugh out bitterly. This was the exact thing she wanted to avoid. Was she really about to choose between her love and her family? Is it a choice? Like Kang-Dae said, there was no certainty in that water, with him there could be. Staring into his equally watery and loving eyes, she unconsciously took a step forward. She watched as a flash of hope came upon his face.

"Do it!" Yoon's voice shouted it out.

Serenity stumbled back. It felt like she'd been pushed. As she looked down at the protruding dagger in her chest her head tilted in confusion. She looked at Kang-Dae whose face was white. The pain wasn't immediate, it was her legs that went out first. Before she could fall completely, she grabbed onto the guard, pulling him with her as she fell back off the ridge. Kang-Dae's anguished screams were all she heard as she hit the water. Just as darkness took her, her last thoughts were of him. 'I could have been happy here. I could have been happy with you.'

CHAPTER SIXTY-TWO

"Serenity! Serenity!" Kang-Dae cried out racing to the ledge. Jung-Soo had to tackle him to keep him from going over.

"Let go of me! Let go! We have to get to her!" Jung-Soo struggled, but with Kang-Dae's wild movements he was slowly losing his grip. "Arezoo!" Jung-Soo called out. Arezoo was staring at the lake, frozen. "AREZOO!!!" Jolting her from her shock, she turned to him. "Help me!" She raced over. Using her fingers, she quickly hit the right pressure points on the King's neck. He was unconscious in seconds. Jung-Soo panted as he slowly released Kang-Dae. He stood up and wiped at his nose. When his hands felt wetness, he realized he was crying.

"Have some men get some nets together and a boat. We need to pull her out. No one can go in themselves," he ordered, wiping at his eyes.

"She's not there," Arezoo spoke up.

Jung-Soo looked at her. "I saw her fall. But I saw something else- something bright beneath the surface. It was quick, but I saw it. She's not there."

Jung-Soo let out a harsh wavering breath. His grief wrapped around him.

"It had to be done," Yoon spoke, drawing both his and Arezoo's attention. "She was abandoning the King and the country. She had denounced her throne. That is treason of the highest order. Death is the only suitable punishment."

Arezoo moved to draw her sword, but Jung-Soo stopped her. "The law will be on my side. Now that she is gone, the King must adhere to council law." Jung-Soo walked over to him.

"You can arrest me, but the nobles will agree. No man can find me guilty. This was justi-." Yoon's words were lost under the choking sounds coming from his throat. Jung-Soo twisted his sword in the man's gut, making him gurgle.

"Guilty," was all Jung-Soo said, looking him in the eyes before yanking his blade out. Yoon held his gaping wound as his blood overflowed in his hands. His paling face filled with pain and fear as struggled to breathe in his last moments.

"Get the King. We're going home." Jung-Soo announced, voice heavy with emotion.

***

The voices were far away. She could hear them, but she couldn't make out what they were saying. Drifting in and out of darkness, Serenity struggled to open her eyes, but she couldn't. Kang-Dae. She wanted Kang-Dae.

"Wake up, baby. That's it. We're right here." Her mother's voice sounded so clear and close. "Go get your father, tell him she's waking up! Open your eyes, baby."

The light was too bright, it made her want to keep them closed. She tried to turn away from it, but her head felt so heavy. She eventually managed to open her eyes. Her mother's tear-stained face was the first thing she saw. "Hey, baby," she greeted.

"Mama," she croaked out.

"Shh, it's alright you don't have to talk now. I'm just glad you're awake."

"Wh-where-," she struggled to speak.

"You're at the hospital. The police finally found you and brought you here. You were hurt pretty badly, but the doctors got to you in time."

Serenity squeezed her mom's hand. "It's okay, baby. I 'm right here. You're home now." Tears welled up in Serenity's eyes. She was home. She had made it back, but the happiness she felt was followed by intense grief. She began to sob. "Oh, it's okay, honey. I've got you. Everything's gonna be alright now."

'No,' she thought. It wasn't going to be alright. Even though she'd finally made it home, she'd left her heart behind.

End Book 2

Book 3

The King's Seer: Intertwining Destiny

Serenity's made it home, all should be well. But that is far from true. Despite being back with the family she so desperately fought to return to, all she can think about is the life she left behind. Her aching heart grows worse day by day, but she doesn't have anyone to confide in about her impossible adventure. So, she keeps it all to herself, letting her grief slowly consume her.

With no seer, no queen, and no love of his life, Kang-Dae is in a bad place. Though those around him try to convince him Serenity is gone for good, he refuses to accept it. There's something inside him that desperately clings to the hope that she is alive. His kingdom needs him, yet he can't help feeling Serenity needs him more. The only thing he can think of is getting her back… and he's willing to cross worlds to do so.

Made in the USA
Columbia, SC
08 January 2025

51406190R00257